Holding on

Past generations of the Gordon-Fenns made their wealth in trade, but their descendants – Samuel, his effete son Edward and his wife Edith – live in much reduced circumstances due to their own mismanagement and the effect of inflation upon the family fortune. But they cling to snobbish values and a belief that privileges which have certainly not been earned by their own efforts should, nevertheless, be theirs by virtue of inherited right. They live in a large, decaying house, in a morass of inactivity. Grandfather Samuel, however, is always 'busy' – writing letters to the government about the deplorable state of the country and the Blacks – letters which never arrive, as his granddaughter Felicity buries them in the shrubbery after carefully removing the stamps.

Grandfather's other preoccupation is in plotting to evict Lily Gudgeon, the gardener's widow, from her cottage, so that he can sell the land for development.

Felicity, left to her own underhand devices and her own moral standards, also becomes involved in the harassment of Lily Gudgeon. A complex cat-and-mouse game develops, in which each side at one time appears to be winning. But Mrs Gudgeon and her shady companion hold the trump card, which turns this witty, beautifully written black comedy into a hauntingly obsessive story.

Eva Hanagan has written three previous novels of which *The Upas Tree* was most recently published :
'Providing continuous pleasure . . . a theme treated with humour and originality. A fine book' David Cook, *New Statesman*. 'Precise and witty writing turn *The Upas Tree* into a delight.' Thomas Hinde *Sunday Telegraph*. 'A very funny novel.' *Glasgow Herald*.

In Thrall (her first novel) :
'So beautifully and precisely visualised that I too was enthralled . . . a delicious piece of water-colour gothic.' Michael Maxwell-Scott *Daily Telegraph*.

By the same author

In thrall
Playmates
The Upas tree

Holding on

a novel by

Eva Hanagan

Eva Hanagan (signature)

Constable London

First published in Great Britain in 1980
by Constable and Company Limited
10 Orange Street London WC2H 7EG
Copyright © by Eva Hanagan 1980
ISBN 0 09 463300 2
Set in Linotype Pilgrim 11 pt
Printed in Great Britain by The Anchor Press Ltd
and bound by Wm Brendon & Son Ltd
both of Tiptree, Essex

To my brothers
Hamish and Alistair Ross

1

'The bloody woman's going gaga – off her silly head!'
Samuel Gordon-Fenn tossed the letter from him and, like
a flat stone dexterously propelled over water, it planed down
the glacial surface of the breakfast table and came to rest
only when one corner was trapped in the marmalade dish.

Samuel had been staring at the letter for some minutes
before pronouncing on the state of mind of its sender and
his son had seized the opportunity to slide the folded newspaper from its place at the side of the old man's plate to a
position from which he could read at least the first para-
graphs of the front-page lead story. There were occasions,
Edward reflected, when the growing improvement in his
long sight did prove to be an advantage. But it was ironical
that the deterioration in one's near sight and the accompany-
ing improvement in one's long sight should occur at that
period in one's life when (realising the unlikelihood of ever
attaining them) one had ceased to fix one's eyes on distant
goals. His optician had assured him that these changes were
normal manifestations of the onset of middle age – as though
that, in itself, was not legitimate cause for concern!

The letter, Felicity could see, had come from Mrs Gudgeon,
the bright blue hue of the paper was instantly recognisable.
Mrs Gudgeon's letters invariably irritated Grandfather. There
were few things which did not irritate Grandfather and these,
such as they were, he chose to ignore as though he recognised
that irritation was his life force and that without constant
refuelling he might seize up altogether. Felicity would have
liked to have been able to read the letter but it had landed
face down; she would also have liked to point out to her

grandfather that, as he had been declaring for years that Lily Gudgeon was mad, it was illogical to state now that she was *going* mad. But she had learned that it was wiser not to contradict Grandfather; even agreement was dangerous as it only encouraged him to expound his opinions at greater length in case one had overlooked the finer points of the quality of reasoning which had formulated his opinion in the first place. Felicity, although her attention seemed to be concentrated on her boiled egg, had not failed to notice her father's crafty manoeuvre with the newspaper. Why didn't he just appropriate it openly? After all, he paid the newspaper bill. Presumably he saw another copy when he got to the office, but Mother never saw the paper at all until it had been retrieved, a day later, from Grandfather's room — and by that time it had been so mutilated and had had so many pieces cut out that it barely hung together.

Samuel's brown blotched hand thudded down on the newspaper and dragged it back in to his own territorial space at the head of the table.

'I despise you,' Edward heard his daughter say, although he knew that in fact she had said nothing – at least not aloud. It was strange how Felicity sometimes communicated with him without having actually to utter a word. Appalled as he was by these occasional remarks and the uncanny circumstance of their silent transmission, Edward found it less frightening to believe that his twelve-year-old daughter did communicate with him in some weird fashion than to face the possibility that the utterances were simply figments of his own imagination.

Samuel glanced at a headline – 'Dustbin men coming out on strike again, or should I say "the cleansing operatives are about to withhold their labour"!' Despite the heavy sarcasm of his tone, he sounded pleased, almost triumphant, at this further evidence of the truth of his frequently voiced opinion that the country was going to the dogs.

'They're cunning buggers,' he continued, stabbing the air with his fork from which drooped a strip of fatty bacon, 'you've got to grant them that! Call their strike at a time when the rubbish will stink. A plague of rats, flies, disease, diarrhoea!' He chomped on the bacon and jabbed at the fried egg whose yolk oozed from under a slobber of raw albumen. 'You've got a wife in a thousand, Edward. Can't be many women incapable of frying an egg!'

Quite true, thought Edith. But, that being so, why did Samuel insist on having a bacon-and-egg breakfast when the rest of the household had long been converted to the simpler, and decidedly more economical, alternative of a boiled egg? He had made a great issue of it, declaring that an Englishman had an undisputed right to enjoy a substantial breakfast; indulgence in grilled kidneys, mushrooms, kedgeree and even the undemanding sausage he was prepared to renounce out of consideration for Edith's deplorable lack of domestic help in the kitchen – but at the sacrifice of bacon and egg he drew a line. The trouble with the middle class, Samuel had declared, was that they had apparently long forgotten that lines *had* to be drawn. Edith had tried to bring him back to the comparatively minor matter under discussion (never an easy task as Samuel preferred to think in terms of what he described as 'the wider issues at stake'), and had pointed out to him the exorbitant price of bacon. That, he had loftily declared, was beyond his control, although he had tried to avert that and many another price increase by wholeheartedly throwing his weight behind the Anti-Common Market Movement. The outcome of Britain putting herself in the hands of conniving foreigners had, to Samuel, been a foregone conclusion. Besides, he had added, the manner in which she conducted the management of her household expenditure was quite outside his province and so long as such control did not interfere with his right to a bacon-and-egg breakfast, he had no intention of infringing upon her domestic authority.

Edward, in helping himself to some marmalade, had lifted the letter and was now reading it and permitting himself the slight twitch of his lips which was as much as he ever displayed by way of a smile. Edith's eye caught it and she was duly grateful, as the sight was a rare one and so not to be missed. Samuel had spotted it too and, as affronted as though his son had thrown himself about in a paroxysm of unseemly mirth, demanded – 'What's so almighty comic then about clear evidence that I have to deal with a madwoman – have to try to knock reason into the head of a woman who is obviously so deranged that she sends a letter which is only a beginning and an ending with no content in between? Where's the joke there – unless you find madness funny, and even in these deplorable times I would have thought that a pretty caddish sort of amusement!'

Edward fastidiously wiped the marmalade from the corner of the letter. Damn, thought Edith, surely it wasn't asking too much that napkins should be expected to last a week between washings – if Edward had the ironing of them, he'd be more careful.

'But it *is* a letter, Father! Don't you see, she's put a full stop there – not a comma!' Holding the letter at arm's length, he read it aloud. ' "Dear Sir, I remain." Full stop there, d'you see? "Yours faithfully, Lily Gudgeon". She has said exactly what she intends to convey. Rather amusing, really!'

'More tea, anybody?' Edith grasped the teapot and smiled fixedly at no one in particular. It was really too bad of Edward; he would escape from the house for the rest of the day, as would Felicity, but she would be left alone to cope with Samuel's rage. He was already turning a very disagreeable colour and his eyes were popping alarmingly. He looked positively apocalyptic – or was it apoplectic? Really it was little wonder that her mind stumbled over words, the wonder was that she retained a modicum of sanity at all. It would carry him off one day, an apoplectic fit. As long as he did go quickly, just 'pop' as the word suggested, it would be all right; but he might linger, a great, growling, helpless hulk for her to dance attendance on. Edward really should consider that before he set off one of his father's tantrums.

Samuel grabbed the letter, crushed it into a ball and flung

it up and away from him. It fell to rest among the scorched moths and brittle dead flies in the frosted glass bowl that hung from brass chains below the central light.

'And you find that funny, do you? Amusing, is it, that an impertinent bitch can shelter behind the damn-fool legislation imposed by the scoundrels and incompetents who run the country? What kind of justice is there in a man being prevented from disposing of his own property as he pleases, eh? Just answer me that, if you can.' But Samuel did not wait for an answer, but roared on, 'It's plain as a pikestaff that the cottage is mine, *mine*, d'you hear – so I should have the right to do what I damn well please with it. Empty it, sell it, set fire to it, if I have a mind to! The idiots who pass the laws in this country allow that . . . that woman . . . to laugh up her sleeve at me. She thinks that she can be smart at my expense, well I'll . . . I'll . . . !' Samuel heaved himself to his feet, resting his weight on his thick, heavy hands, the fingers splayed like pork sausages on the mahogany. He thrust his engorged face towards his son.

'Haven't you the wit to see that it's your financial prospects, as much as mine, that she's playing ducks and drakes with? Or do you just not bloody care – apathetic as the rest of your mealy-mouthed generation? Call yourself a solicitor – God help us!' He dropped heavily back into his chair with the air of a man temporarily silenced by the sheer stupidity of his audience. He heaved a theatrical sigh which turned into a belch.

'I have explained, Father,' Edward was folding his napkin, meticulously aligning the creases. 'It's not as easy as you seem to think.'

But Samuel was not listening. He had clamped a hand to his stomach, 'Ulcers, that's what that creature's sheer bloody-mindedness has brought me to!'

'I'll fetch your bismuth.' Edith rose, glad of the excuse to leave the room and relieved that Samuel had slipped into another key. His bouts of self-pity were tiresome but preferable to his moods of fulminating fury. He didn't have a duodenal ulcer, Edith knew that, but it was wiser not to challenge the assertion. Considering his gluttony and prodigous capacity for the outpouring of rancour, he certainly deserved to suffer from ulcers but, reflected Edith as she searched among the pickle jars for the medicine bottle, life was random with its rewards and punishments and rarely handed them out on the basis of what was deserved. The day that he had returned from the surgery where he had heard the results of the hospital tests, Samuel had declared that the Health Service was run by quacks, charlatans and conniving coons and that Dr Carey was an incompetent poop incapable of diagnosing nappy rash on a baby's bum. As he refused to discuss exactly what the outcome of the tests had been, Edith had telephoned the surgery and had been told that her father-in-law suffered only from the symptoms of swallowed air. The doctor had added that it would be no bad thing if Samuel could be persuaded to cut down on his food intake and cultivate a more sanguine approach to life. But Dr Carey's voice had conveyed no hope that his advice would be heeded – after all, he had been Samuel's practitioner for many years.

Edith was still stirring the mixture in the glass when she heard Edward and Felicity call out their perfunctory goodbyes from the hall. She was sure that, at that age, she had never left for school without giving Mumsie a kiss; but Felicity was just not that sort of a child. Perhaps, she reflected, it was a good thing, on the whole, that Felicity was not a sensitive, dependent sort of a child, but a quiet, self-sufficient one. Felicity was a bit like a peasant who had been born and bred on the slopes of a volcano and went placidly about her daily living, undismayed by the intermittent quaking of the earth below her feet and the recurrent grumbling and roaring from above; and, of course, she had the confidence of youth and an instinctive awareness that if and when an eruption came, she could run away. That must be a nice feeling, thought Edith, to know that there were other fields, not overhung with threat, and time enough to reach them.

'Don't slouch!'

Edward heard the testy tone in his voice and regretted the admonition as soon as it had been uttered. But Felicity *was* slouching, slumped beside him in the car, her arms wrapped around the schoolbag on her knees and her legs sprawled all anyhow. Little wonder, he excused himself, if he did sound irritable – his father would try the patience of a saint.

Felicity did not deign to alter her posture apart from turning her head to stare out of the window. He should try to talk to her, Edward told himself, really talk, not just make remarks; but it wasn't easy to talk to the back of a straw boater. What went on under that hat, inside that sleekly-haired skull, behind those eyes that held such an uncanny resemblance to those of his long-dead mother? Not much of Edith in Felicity – peculiar that, but people did say that likeness often skipped a generation; at least he thought he'd heard that said.

Edward swerved to avoid a sauntering cat.

'You missed it!' Felicity exclaimed. But surely that was not a note of reproach in her voice? Surprise, more likely. Surprise that he could do anything successfully. Edward checked himself, he was thinking quite irrationally; it was just that one brought expectations to fatherhood. One hoped, foolishly no doubt, that one's child would be a comfort, an ally. Nonsense, of course. He had never achieved an easy relationship with his own father, so why should he expect his own child to act any differently towards himself? Edith said that Felicity was 'approaching a difficult age' – just as though there existed an age which was otherwise! But Edith probably was right. Things would improve with time – not that that had been borne out by Edward's experience of life to date, but he had not entirely given up hope.

'Well, here we are!' Edward announced with forced brightness as he drew up at the entrance to Felicity's school. He leant across his daughter to open the door for her, but she had the catch down before him and, without a backward glance, was through the gates before he had drawn away from the kerb. Her father dismissed her from his mind and turned his thoughts to the grievances which the day to come undoubtedly held in store.

When Edith returned to the dining-room with his medicine, it was to find that Samuel was no longer there. She climbed the front stairs noting the dust that filmed the white paint-work on either side of the worn Turkey carpet and hoped that when Mrs Watson came she would be in a mood to accept a hint; it always had to be a hint rather than an instruction. One had to be tactful where Mrs Watson was concerned.

She knocked on the door of what Samuel chose to call his Office. A corner room and quite the largest and sunniest on the first floor of Westwood, it still subtly bore the imprint of a bedroom although the bed and the rest of the furnishings appropriate to a bedroom had been moved into the connecting dressing-room. Perhaps it was the curtains with their delicate roses-on-a-trellis design that were the give-away. Samuel was standing by the window and had not bothered to turn round when she had knocked. He knew it could only be Edith because, although this was one of Mrs Watson's days and, for all he knew, she might for once have arrived on time, she would not have the temerity to knock or to expect admission to Samuel's Office – she had learned better than that!

There was a droop to his shoulders and, seen like that, from the back and in silence, it would be quite easy to feel sorry for him. 'What was Samuel really *for*,' Edith wondered, not for the first time, and, what was more puzzling, 'what did *he* think he was for?' But she saw the way Samuel's hand was grasping the edge of the curtain, dragging and puckering the fabric where it was already thin with decades of im-patient drawing, and allowed irritation to overcome any more dangerous emotion.

14

'I've brought you your bismuth,' she said, placing the glass on the desk so that he would have to release the curtain.

'Thank you, my dear, thank you. I don't know how I'd get along without you. Can't be easy for you, running this bloody mausoleum on a shoe-string – and Edward's a bit of a broken reed.' He'd gulped down the bismuth and a whitish scum clung to his moustache. 'Sorry, shouldn't have said that. You'd be the last to criticise him. Quite right too! Loyalty – that's what you've got, girl, loyalty! Not much of that around, more's the pity. Loyalty, honour, decency – all trampled underfoot these days.' She reached out for the empty glass and he clamped his hand on her arm, the sun from the window behind him gilding the wiry hairs on his wrist so that they glistened like the bristles on a hog's back. 'You're a good girl, Edith; a good girl!'

'Your dark suit will need a press if you're going up to town tomorrow.'

'Ah yes,' he released her arm and flicked open the large leather-bound appointments book on his desk with the resigned air of a busy man whose life was beset with engagements. 'Hmmmm, AGM Wednesday, 11 a.m. Quite right, my dear, clever of you to remember!'

She could hardly have forgotten. Samuel transcribed his engagements from his desk diary to her memo-board in the kitchen every Monday morning without fail – just when she was busy sorting out the week's washing. He wrote boldly, frequently breaking the point off the chinograph pencil, and with complete disregard for her own cryptic shopping-list reminders. 'Wednesday a.m. AGM London. SEE TO SUIT' had quite overrun 'sago, take Edward's shoes for re-heeling'. But the message had brightened her Monday gloom as intimation of his absence for a whole day invariably did. It would be her chance, too, to give his rooms a good going-over.

'I'll hang the suit on my bedroom doorknob – your woman can come up and fetch it.'

'Your woman' indeed! Edith pursed her lips with exasperation as she closed the door behind her. Oh the smell in that room! Stale tobacco smoke and mice. Samuel wouldn't admit to the mice but Edith just knew they were there; she'd even found droppings on the carpet and placed them on his desk, but he'd insisted that they were crumbled dottles from his pipe. And then there were the musty-smelling piles of old periodicals and the smaller drifts of handwritten notes, his papers he called them. Oh God, what was the use!

Samuel was casting a satisfied eye over his papers now. Yes, there was a whole morning's filing there without a doubt and, of course, today's paper to be gone through. Little sheafs of newspaper cuttings were ranged down one side of the big table in the centre of the room, each pile anchored with a glass paperweight. Edwina had given them to him over the years as birthday presents with, he'd sometimes thought at the time, almost boring predictability. The first paper-weight, presented to him on his first birthday after their marriage, had been accompanied by a little card on which Edwina had written, 'This reminds me of you, my darling. Under the surface there is a mystery which I cannot reach or touch.' Rum sort of thing to have written, Samuel had thought at the time; but there had been a romantic, fanciful streak in Edwina. She was a woman, after all, and women were subject to that sort of thing. But he'd rather liked the thought of being a man of hidden depths. Some time, reflected Samuel, he really must have their value updated and entered in his ledger of personal assets. It was finding the time to fit all these little tasks into his work schedule that was the problem. Pity there were only nineteen of them, twenty would have been a nice rounded number for a collection. It had been just after the war that she had stopped giving them to him. It had quite thrown him to find a larger than usual, and rectangular, parcel by his breakfast plate. For years he had made the same little joke of pretending not to know what could be inside the little ribbon-tied box, and then affected exaggerated surprise to find it contained yet another glass paperweight. That year he had not had to simulate puzzlement as he had turned the parcel over in his hands and expressed the familiar formula of, 'Now, what have we got here, I wonder?' Half a dozen golf balls had turned out to be the astonishing answer. Very acceptable really, golf balls had still been hard to come by so soon after the end of the war. But strange, all the same. Edwina had not really explained, had just said, lightly, 'I think you should be encouraged to spend more time on the golf course and less in the garden.' She'd never bought him another paperweight after that.

That concoction which Edith had brought him had left a deuced unpleasant taste in his mouth; pepperminty, brought back the ghost of Sundays past. Samuel took a key from an inner pocket, swivelled his chair a little so that his belly no longer obscured the lock and opened the central desk drawer from which he extracted the key that opened the side drawers. Carefully he unlocked all the drawers, taking a small bunch of keys from the top right one and laying them in the centre of his blotter; these were the keys to the metal filing cabinets and, presently, he would unlock them, pulling each drawer fractionally open, an arrangement which gave to the room a purposeful, busy air – or so it seemed to Samuel. From the deep bottom left-hand drawer of the desk he withdrew a bottle of Scotch, a glass and a packet of digestive biscuits. Puffing a little from the exertion of bending, he poured himself out a generous tot and refilled his pipe.

That's much better, he thought, swilling the whisky round his molars and flushing out the last gritty grains of bismuth. Edith clearly had not stirred with sufficient care to dissolve all the powder. That was one of Edith's faults, always in a rush, skimping things, muddling through. She had that sort of look about her, harried; if she didn't look out she could well develop a shrewish expression in age. Always that danger with slim women with finely boned faces. But, in all honesty, Samuel reflected as he blew a lilac smoke ring towards the ceiling, Edith was skinny rather than slim. Edwina had been slim; trim boyish flanks and lovely legs that had gone on for ever; not much of a bosom, but then that hadn't been the thing way back in the Twenties. Funny how women could change their shapes to suit the fashion of the day! But Edwina had had elegance even in the days when she had worn ridiculous short, shapeless dresses and her head, hidden under a cloche hat, had been thrust forward in the slink that had been all the rage at that time. Yes, that was what Edwina had had, elegance. Now that was another thing that had gone – elegance. No elegant women around nowadays. Sloppily dressed women tramped around the streets in hideous clumsy shoes, big bottoms wobbling in ghastly trousers. No delicacy, no *gamin* allure. There were the boots some of them wore, too – God, the boots really disgusted him! At least Edith didn't go in for those, most likely a matter of economy though. Edith never seemed to spend much on clothes. Not that it mattered really, Edith wasn't the sort for whom clothes could do much, if one thought about it. Now Edwina, on the other hand, had suffered when things got financially tight and she had no longer been able to splash out on clothes. She'd done her best with what could be afforded, of course, but the sparkle had started to go out of her about then – must have been in the mid-Thirties. Yes, 1935, to be exact. That had been the year when everything had started to go wrong and they'd had to give up the London house and come back here to Westwood and Mother. Mother hadn't helped – she and Edwina had never hit it off. No two ways about it, it had been downhill all the way after that.

Samuel poured himself another drink to take the taste of the past away. He recapped the bottle and put it away in the drawer, reminding himself that it had to last out until the end of the week.

With a foot he dragged a chair closer to the desk and heaved his legs on to it, lifting them with his hands under the thighs to make the manoeuvre easier. Not a bad thing, he told himself, to relax a bit after breakfast; gave the digestion a chance to work properly and afforded a reflective interval in which to plan the day's work schedule. This morning

priority would have to be give to a final study of the balance
sheet of Universal Toiletries in preparation for tomorrow's
Annual General Meeting. Then there was a letter to be written
to the local paper drawing attention to Trotskyist infiltra-
tion in Local Government. That should go off today if it was
to catch this week's edition – always assuming that the editor
would publish it. He was a singularly obstructive man, the
editor, thought Samuel, frowning as he recalled various
acrimonious and counter-productive telephone conversations.
Youngest son of the local fishmonger, which probably
accounted for his arrogance, jumped-up nobody that he was,
wielding petty authority and drunk with his own power!
That was part of the root of the troubles in today's society,
too many people in positions of power who had not been
brought up to shoulder the burdens of responsibility. Samuel
was pleased with the sound of that and made a note of it on a
sheet of paper which he then placed in a wire tray marked
'Matters awaiting attention'. Last week's Sunday papers had
still not come under his scissors, and the matter of Lily
Gudgeon required attention. He groaned a little and chomped
on a digestive biscuit for comfort.

'You ought to get yourself a dishwasher, it's not as though
you don't have the room for one.' Mrs Watson, dazzling in
flowered acrylic, was busy making the pot of tea without
which she never felt properly 'set-up' for a morning's work.
'Now, poor Mrs Cardew had a terrible job getting hers fitted
in; had to have the tumble drier moved up one end and the
units all rearranged. But it was worth it in the end! A real
boon, she says it is.'

Edith clattered the dishes more loudly than was necessary
in the sink where Mrs Watson had thoughtfully stacked them
for her. Mrs Cardew was Mrs Watson's Monday and Friday
lady and Miss Frewin, who commuted daily to London on
business and whose sheets matched her curtains and whose
pictures were the real thing and not any of your cheap

reproductions, engaged that lady's services on Wednesdays. Edith was personally acquainted with neither, and heartily resented both.

Behind her, she could hear the biscuit tin rattle as Mrs Watson's fat fingers poked about. 'You're getting low on the bourbons,' she said, peevishly. 'Don't worry, luv, I'll add it to your list!' While Mrs Watson's back was turned, Edith took her cup of tea from the table and placed it beside herself on the draining board; better to drink it standing up with her soapy fingers skidding on the cup handle than to sit down at the table in a show of intimacy with Mrs Watson. Not that these subtle intimations of line-drawing seemed to impinge on Mrs Watson's awareness, or, if they did, she chose generously to ignore them.

'He's out tomorrow then!' Mrs Watson, having scrawled 'Burbones' in uncertain capitals on the board, was reading the other notices with interest. 'I'll get the iron on for his suit. I may have to give the morning-room the go-by but p'raps I'll catch up on Thursday.'

Edith yanked out the sink plug. So, she'd have to do the morning-room herself tomorrow as well as Samuel's room. There would be the stairs too – they really couldn't be left longer in that state. The wonder was that Edward hadn't said something about their condition; not that he ever actually *said* anything, he just stared in a pained sort of way or squiggled a finger through the dust. At least she thought it was Edward who was responsible for the strange, almost cabalistic, signs that appeared on surfaces from time to time. She had never actually caught him at it, but surely it could only be Edward who was responsible; unless it was his grandmother who flitted back to Westwood from time to time to see how things were going without her and felt impelled to register her disapproval. Dora, if her portrait was a faithful likeness, looked the fault-finding type, but it was hard to imagine her transfigured to an ethereal role. A woman of presence, that was what Dora must have been, but immediate presence, surely, not lingering. Whatever spirit pervaded

Westwood it could scarcely be described as one of purpose and vigour.

Her hands still dangling in the draining sink, Edith had been standing for longer than she dared guess, staring unseeingly out of the kitchen window. She could hear the hum of the vacuum cleaner from the direction of the dining-room. Well, that was something! Mrs Watson had actually got down to things. Samuel was tucked away and occupied for the rest of the morning – for the whole of the day, with any luck. She could go out and do her customary Tuesday shopping. It was not that Edith enjoyed the actual shopping, but any legitimate reason for getting out of the house was welcome.

She sat down at the table and began to write out her list, rising from time to time to check the store cupboard, the refrigerator and the memo-board. Someone possessed of a more methodical approach would not have required to make quite so many trips, clickety-clack across the worn linoleum, but Edith would have been the last person to lay claim to being efficiently organised.

The list completed, she made a rough calculation of its total cost, crossed out a few items and placed query marks against others. Some day, she promised herself, she really would send Samuel to do the shopping. Oh, he ranted and bellowed about inflation, aired his opinions as to its cause and cure, but seemed unwilling, or unable, to appreciate its immediate and practical impact. 'Come and share Westwood with me!' he had urged all those years ago when Edwina had died. Thirteen years ago, to be exact, she reminded herself sourly; the calculation had not been difficult because Felicity had been born just over a year after they had made the move. At first things had seemed financially easier and even Edward had cautiously agreed that perhaps they might at last launch a family. The surge of optimism had rapidly receded, or perhaps the advent of a baby after eight years of prudent procrastination had proved too much of an upheaval to invite repetition. Whatever the reason, the concept of a family and the plurality intimated by the word had not again been referred to by Edward.

'Think of the advantages,' Samuel had enthused, 'no rent to pay, naturally – wouldn't dream of expecting anything of the sort from my own son! Sell your little house, no mortgage round your necks, a little bit of capital to hand after redemption!' Well, he'd kept his word. They paid no rent. But they did pay the rates, the fuel bills and practically every other running cost incurred by living in a run-down Victorian house which was heir to all the discomforts and inconveniences peculiar to its type. Edward had entertained doubts as to the wisdom of making their home with his father, but these had been overruled by the concern he felt at the change which had been wrought in Samuel by the years of Edwina's decline and, finally, by her death. 'Decline' was the word used by both Samuel and Edward when referring to Edwina's condition and Edith, too, came to adopt it; 'decline' was a safe word, respectable, almost graceful, carrying an inference of a gently fading flower. 'He's a broken man, Edith. We can't just leave him alone there, rattling about in Westwood with nothing to look forward to but lonely old age and death.' Well, broken Samuel might have been but, as it had turned out, certainly not beyond repair.

Whatever had been the nature of the clasps and rivets which Samuel had applied to his psyche in the course of his reassembly, they had effected not only a pulling-together, as it were, but a positive strengthening and reinforcement of the fabric of his personality. Samuel, in short, had become in old age even more objectionable than he had been in youth; a feat the more remarkable for having seemed impossible.

The grandfather clock in the hall gave a tentative bronchial whirr before emitting eleven sonorous booms which penetrated to the kitchen and broke into Edith's reverie with a reminder that it was already ten o'clock and the morning was fast receding. Surely, thought Edith, hurriedly scrambling to her feet, surely it was enough that time in Westwood should either hang tediously or mysteriously accelerate, leaving no tangible evidence of its passing, without the most obtrusive clock in the house adding to the confusion! But until Samuel decided either to sell it or have the clock repaired, nothing would be done. Edward had drawn a line, belatedly but stubbornly; Edward could be very intractable when he chose. The plumber's bill for adjusting the ball cock in the tank in the attic had been the catalyst. Maintenance of services, structural repairs and the mending of furniture which belonged to Samuel would, in future, be Samuel's responsibility, Edward had announced. There had been a horrendous row – at least Samuel had contributed the noise, Edward restricting himself to the pronouncement succeeded by tight-lipped silence. For two years now, Samuel had been quibbling that the grandfather clock was not, strictly speaking, an article of furniture but belonged in the category of 'working equipment'. Edward had not, at least as yet, expected Samuel to foot the bill when the electric kettle had blown its fuse or the flex on the iron needed replacing. Samuel kept a few embers of dissension glowing by tapping the clock occasionally and declaring it would fetch a good price and he had half a mind to sell although doubtless it was increasing in value all the time and would be worth even more to his heir when he was six feet under. But Edward pretended not to hear.

I wonder what they would do, thought Edith, bounding up the backstairs to change her blouse and fetch her handbag, if one day I just screamed and screamed? But she knew that she would never put them to the test, suspecting, as she did, that only grievance and unarticulated anger provided the strength that kept her at minimum flight distance from absolute despair. Really, I'm running on the spot, she thought, reaching the top of the stairs slightly out of breath.

Mrs Watson was in the kitchen when Edith returned downstairs. She was spreading Samuel's black trousers out on the ironing-board and peering at the crotch in a very intrusive manner. 'They're on their last legs!' she volunteered, and then, with her laugh that sounded like the bark of a jackal and always set off her smoker's cough, added, 'Funny that, eh? Trousers on their last legs!' Edith hurried out, leaving Mrs Watson clutching the ironing-board and gasping for air like a beached porpoise. She'll stop working now and make herself another pot of tea as soon as I've gone, 'to ease her tubes'. Well, thought Edith, there's nothing I can do to prevent her wasting her time and my money. Edith gave the garage door a vicious kick, but not entirely out of malice; the action was necessary to operate the lock which had long since refused to respond to a key or to gentle persuasion.

Still, she thought, having backed out and turned the car to face down the drive (a manoeuvre requiring some care if she was not to scrape Mrs Watson's impeccable scarlet Mini), the garden really does look beautiful. The front garden, that is, she amended, refusing even to think about the wilderness that stretched out behind Westwood. Above the idling engine a blackbird's song rippled the air. He was perched on a guelder rose, silhouetted against the cascade of white blossom, the branch gently swinging under his tiny weight. Singing fit to burst his heart, just as though everything in the garden really was lovely – well, perhaps it was from his viewpoint. Lucky bird.

It was the ease of its upkeep that prevented this part of the garden from degenerating into the state of tangled neglect that had overtaken the rest of the grounds. The lawn, brilliant in the first flush of its spring growth, was bordered by a wide half-circle of flowering shrubs. Potentillas frilled the edges with a froth of yellow blossom and, behind and above them, rose long-established bushes of camellia, their blossoms singing out against the dark foliage in every note on the scale of pink from shell to vibrant crimson. A sprinkling of cherry blossom stirred gently on the grass. Edith frowned slightly, there were other white flecks there, not fallen blossom but daisies. Agreeable though the milkman was, to keep the lawn mowed for a reasonable payment, would she be putting a strain on the arrangement if she asked him to keep the daisies down? Did they matter so much, the daisies, the dust on the stairs? But if petty details like that did not matter, then, in some subtle way, the whole relevance of the fabric of her existence was threatened.

Edith released the handbrake and coasted down the drive and wished that, on this glorious May morning, her goal was not the supermarket. There had been a time when shopping had been almost a pleasure. But that seemed a distant period now; the early years of her married life when they had lived in Winchester and she had shopped in friendly, old-fashioned shops where an attentive assistant had written down one's order, prompting one respectfully if one had omitted an item of regular purchase; an assistant who had seemed genuinely concerned that the Cheddar would be just right for one's requirements, proferring little cubes on a square of grease-proof paper so that one could assess at one's leisure its degree of mildness or strength. One had one's identity confirmed as the assistant headed the order form with one's name and address from memory because one was known, recognised, greeted with courtesy and a degree of respect which was indisputably gratifying. One was young Mrs Gordon-Fenn whose order was never extravagant but was treated, none the less, with caring attention and delivered promptly. Edith glared icily at a young man on a motorbike who had cheekily overtaken her on the inside and stuck his tongue out at her in passing; perhaps she was driving rather close to the crest of the road, but there was no call for that sort of behaviour! Money had certainly been tight in those days too, she reflected, allowing her attention to drift again. But the need for economy had been cheerfully accepted. Edward, after all, was still on the first rungs of his profession; in time things would improve – that had seemed a natural assumption. Edward was diligent and deserved to get on. That was what she had thought. But Edward had proved to be but a plodder, timid, lacking both ambition and inspiration. Edward did not get on. Instead, Edward had returned to the decaying nest of Westwood and a junior partnership in an unsuccessful firm of solicitors where his lack of drive was admirably suited to the prevailing tempo.

But, thought Edith, waiting for the traffic lights to change, even if we still lived in our dear little house in Winchester, things would have changed there, too, over the years. I expect that grocer's shop has gone, not even the scent of roasting coffee-beans left lingering on the air. It had probably been turned into a shoe shop or an Electricity Board showroom.

She left her car in the gloomy bowels of the high-rise car park. Gagging from the reek of petrol and exhaust fumes, her eyes averted from the crude graffiti scrawled on the dark, damp-streaked walls, she rushed for the open air, dragging her shopping trolley behind her and narrowly escaping slipping to the concrete floor on a slick of stinking oil.

Now for the next horror, she told herself, filling her lungs with the relatively mildly polluted air of the High Street and heading for the supermarket.

The familiar panic and confusion overwhelmed her as soon as she crossed the entrance where the door had swung eerily open in advance of her entry. Inside, the noises were inhuman, such sounds as were of human origin being swamped by the rattle of metal trolleys and the clatter of cash registers.

'Oh God,' Edith moaned, making her way down aisles flanked by garish displays of shirts, pullovers, pantie-hose and racks of polyester nighties; the food department seemed to get further away on every visit.

A crazed-looking youth was pushing a twenty-foot snake of trolleys straight in her direction, but presumably without malice as his vision was impaired by the shock of hair that straggled over his eyes. Edith jumped awkwardly out of the way, rushed blindly down the first opening she saw and found herself, by some miracle, in the aisle which she had sought. Or so it appeared at first sight; but another disconcerting feature of the supermarket was that nothing remained constant.

26

They had been on those shelves last week, Edith was almost sure of that: sago, lentils, rice . . . but now, not a cereal or a pulse was in sight. In their place was a display of Easter eggs. Surely Easter was over and done with . . . or was it? reflected Edith uneasily, no longer trusting in her own memory. Yes, apparently it was, she decided with a relief, observing now that the display was overhung by a huge scarlet hare clutching in his teeth a sign which declared 'Reduced'. He was wearing a top hat. The Mad March Hare, perhaps? But he had nothing to do with Easter . . . or had he? Already Edith could feel the dithering uncertainty, the sense of disorientation that the supermarket induced in her, taking possession.

Some months previously Edith had had a very disturbing experience, there in the supermarket. She stood now, staring sightlessly ahead as the memory recurred. That particular morning she had worked her way to the far corner of the store where spaghetti, both long and short, pastas and noodles of every imaginable size and shape, were stacked. And then, rounding the last stack of tinned tomatoes, quite unprepared, she had chanced upon that bizarre scene. Two men dressed in brown overalls were carrying a woman between them, one had his hands under her armpits and the other held her by the legs, an ankle grasped in each hand. Between them the woman had slumped, her clothes awry and her face deathly pale. Her eyes had been neither shut nor fully open; the pupils had been rolled up out of sight and only a slit of bloodshot eyeball had gleamed white under the fluorescent lighting. The men were humping her towards a door marked 'Private – Staff Only' and, in seconds, had disappeared behind it. An assistant had appeared, suddenly, at Edith's side and had asked, very brusquely, 'Can I help you?' Edith, too shocked to answer (to be offered assistance was, in itself, a novel and surprising occurrence), had stared back at her, wordlessly. The assistant had then said, loudly and slowly as though addressing a person of patently limited intelligence, 'Are you looking for something?' Edith had been looking for something – macaroni, to be precise. What she had found had been death in the temple of gluttony and greed and that had made her quest seem inappropriate and best left unvoiced. She had walked away, empty-handed. Edward, when she had told him about it, had not shown much interest; had been almost off-hand, in fact. The woman, or so he had said, had probably only fainted, or perhaps she had suffered a fit; such things did happen from time to time. It was not impossible, he had conceded, that the woman had been dead; after all, death was no respecter of convenience or propriety and so, on the law of averages, a few deaths must occur in shops. Edith had scrutinised the local paper that week. There had been no sensational report but in the Deaths column one announcement had had the word 'suddenly' in brackets. Later Edith had wondered if she had really seen anything. She had forced herself to revisit that part of the store. The pastas had disappeared. The shelves had been full of sponge mixes and demerara. But the door was just as she had remembered it; the brown, scuffed door marked 'Private – Staff Only'.

A woman bumped in to her, inflicting a sharp blow on her ankle with a trolley and barked 'Some people!' as she trundled on her way. Edith was suddenly aware that she must have been staring, unintentionally, at a woman who stood a few yards away and who now gave her a tight-lipped scowl, took a tin from her coat pocket and replaced it on the shelf. Edith felt herself blushing. But I haven't done anything, she told herself, taking an Easter egg at random as it seemed a rational thing to appear to be doing in the circumstances. I can always melt it down for chocolate sauce, she told herself, but never mind the wretched sago, I really cannot bear to hunt it down.

She was selecting a piece of brisket, doubled over the frozen-meat cabinet, rootling in its icy depths and trying not to dwell on its mortuary overtones – so white, so cold and so full of dead flesh – when a cross-looking woman barged her aside and grabbed two large packets of fillet steak.

Edith, feeling anger spurt up inside her, walked quickly away and stood in one of the aisles, breathing deeply to dispel a frightening desire to kick something – or, worse still, someone. This time the shelves in front of her were loaded with tins labelled 'Mushy Peas'. Fancy, thought Edith, eager to anchor her thoughts to something harmless, fancy anyone actually wanting to buy peas already mushy. Crazy! She herself could, and frequently did, reduce peas to a mush without incurring any expense at all. A large part of the world is in a state of hunger, Edith told herself, gazing sourly at the loaded shelves, and here one is surrounded by tons and tons of food which is really superfluous to reasonable requirements. No wonder one gets angry! But no, I must face it; the real source of my anger is the rude behaviour of that woman. And it is not only her rudeness which has put me in such a wax but the fact that she was grabbing (and so casually, never a glance at the price labels) two packets of fillet steak which I could not afford. And another thing, Edith told herself, she had looked (well, surely one need not censor one's own thoughts, things had not come to that – not yet), she had looked downright *common*. Edith rubbed her ribs where the woman had shoved her against the edge of the cabinet and allowed self-doubt to surface. On the other hand, she reasoned, why should I think that I have an unassailable (albeit rarely gratified) right to feed my family on fillet steak and that that beastly rude woman ought to be content with mince? Samuel would tell her, without equivocation, that it was because she was a member of the middle class and, as such, had a perfect right to expect to enjoy the best things in life; that was the creed which he preached. But, when it came down to it, what had Samuel himself ever done actually to *earn* that privilege? He had certainly, in his time, kept quite a lot of money in circulation. The truth was that he had squandered money which he had not earned, surely that was hardly a qualification for privilege? And what, thought Edith in a brutal access of self-examination, had she herself done in life that should give her special rights? She

H.O.—B

permitted herself a lesser emotion than anger; she felt peeved, and for that state surely there was justification.

She had done it again, let her eyes rest unthinkingly on someone and now the woman was staring back at her. No, this time it was all right; it was Miranda who was trying to catch her attention by making signs to her from the next aisle. Odd signs – oh yes, she was miming drinking a cup of coffee. Edith waved and nodded and moved quickly away from the mushy peas in case Miranda thought she was about to buy some. There, where the Krispy Krunchy Bacon Nibbles had stood last week, was the sago – well, that was something.

Miranda was already seated at a table in the coffee shop when Edith arrived. She looked pink and cheerful in peach slubbed linen with a chiffon scarf knotted with apparent carelessness at her neck, but the scarf had, in fact, been arranged with some artistry to hide the crêpy skin which failed to respond to moisturising lotions. Miranda looked very expensive and Edith tried to ignore a stab of envy. But then, Miranda could afford to make the best of herself, Godfrey was patently doing well. Accountants always flourished; in times of economic depression they were kept busy with bankruptcies, and in periods of growth there were scarcely enough of them to go round. Edward had patiently explained that to her when Edith had meanly voiced some odious comparison.

Miranda's two children were in an older age group than Felicity and over the years Edith had been treated to regular reports of their progress. It always was progress, except for a slight setback a few years previously when Mary had become a little too intense about religion. But, 'Thank God' as Miranda had put it 'it had been the dear old c. of e. and nothing outlandish like the Moonies or the Scientologists'. The Vicar had been a brick and had helped Mary to get over it completely; but it had been embarrassing while it had lasted.

Jeremy was doing frightfully well in his father's firm and

30

Mary was working hard for her finals and Miranda wouldn't be at all surprised if she pulled off a Double First. Not, of course, Miranda hastened to add, that *that* mattered terribly as long as Mary was happy, she and Godfrey had never put any pressure on their children, just allowed them to find their own level without any stress being imposed upon them.

God, it was all so boring, thought Edith, smiling and nodding from time to time as that was all that was called for. Jeremy was a plump, pompous young man already losing his hair and Mary had none of her mother's looks but had taken after her father, which was not a happy arrangement, but his brains had been part of the package and that was a decided advantage. But Edith did wish sometimes that their lives were a bit less exemplary and a little more exciting – if only to lend interest to their mother's conversation. But not for Jeremy and Mary were little forays into the drug scene, hitch-hiking trips to Kathmandu or exuberant banner-waving at student demonstrations. But, in her heart, Edith longed for just such a dependable, steady progression for Felicity.

Nobody really young in here at all. Edith allowed her gaze to travel over the other coffee sippers while Miranda scrabbled in her bag for Mary's last letter. They all looked dull, thought Edith. Are the interesting ones all busy with jobs, or is it because the coffee drinkers don't have jobs that they seem so unstimulating? Only one woman had a child with her, a youngish woman sitting by the window and frowning at her toddler who was blowing through his straw into his orange squash. One rarely saw babies around now-adays. What had happened, then, to Samuel's prognosticated population explosion? It must have been years ago that he had warned that soon the pavements would be crawling with babies (mostly black), while their mothers crowded into the Post Offices and Social Welfare Offices collecting extravagant hand-outs.

'You're day-dreaming again, Edith! I've never known such a person for drifting off, as you.' Miranda chided, but kindly. She went out of her way to be jolly and entertaining when they met because Edith always looked in need of cheering up. The least Edith could do, surely, was to show a little appreciation and not let her attention wander quite so obviously. It was not as though she ever bored Edith with grumbles and grievances; she had no intention of saying a word about her course of hay-fever injections (which were jolly painful), or anything about Godfrey's dotty old mother who'd started handing out wads of notes to alcoholic down-and-outs. Godfrey was going to have to get a Power of Attorney, it was all very distressing. Mary had been having a terrible time with her periods and Jeremy had his sinusitis back again; but those were precisely the sort of things with which one did not wish to burden Edith, the poor girl had more than enough unpleasantness to cope with at home with that dreadful old man and Edward being such a wet. Felicity seemed quiet enough – as yet. But there was a look about Felicity. She might well grow into a beauty and that gener-ally meant trouble. Never mind, Miranda consoled herself, she was meeting Betty for coffee tomorrow and Betty was always so cheerful and optimistic that one could confide one's anxieties to her with impunity.

'Darling, you haven't forgotten that Betty and I have got the NSPCC thing a week on Saturday? Have you got any jumble for us?'

Well yes, thought Edith, she had. The wardrobes and drawers at Westwood were stuffed with it, the only snag was that most of it was in use.

'I'm not sure,' she replied, and then risked a lie, 'I gave a great pile to the Boy Scouts recently.'

'Oh bother! Something for the bric-à-brac, perhaps?'

Edith looked as though she was giving that some considera-tion but, in fact, she was remembering the frightful row Samuel had made when she'd given Miranda a pair of hideous Benares candlesticks last year. Most of the relics of the family's Indian period which had been of any value had been sold over the years, but Samuel persisted in nursing inflated ideas as to the value and beauty of the oddments that still littered Westwood.

'Nothing that springs to mind.'

'Oh dear, what a shame. People don't seem to be so generous this year; we've had quite a job scraping things together.' Miranda paused, and then added, 'I do hope you don't have the same sort of difficulties that we're having. You have got your bring-and-buy next week, haven't you?' No harm in reminding Edith that one did have obligations, one did have to support one another's charities – if not, where would one be?

She waited a moment for the shaft to sink in; Edith could be a little obtuse at times.

'I've just had a marvellous idea!' Miranda exclaimed, her voice achieving an even higher pitch than usual but still managing to convey the impression that the notion had just occurred to her. 'People are going *mad* about old clothes – doesn't even have to be really antique, just old grotty stuff, pre-war, that sort of thing! Do have a look in your attic, darling, I'll bet there's masses of that kind of junk stuffed away there. There might even be the odd topee or parasol – Samuel's mother's generation never got rid of a thing, if they could help it!'

There certainly were old trunks and boxes up there; Edith had seen them on a once-only and never-to-be-repeated visit. She had gone up to look for a particular canvas chair which Samuel swore was in the attic. She hadn't found the chair, but the search had been cursory as she had found bats. But perhaps she could persuade Felicity to have a look in the boxes.

'Yes, that is an idea – I'll have a look.'

'Super! Give me a ring and I'll come and collect. I know you won't let me down. By the way, I saw the oddest thing this morning, packets of desiccated coconut and the spelling was wrong – two s's and one c, can you imagine!'

'Perhaps it was just a printing mistake?' Edith hazarded, not at all sure herself as to how to spell the word.

'Not a bit of it, darling! It's the terrible education in the schools today. They're turning out illiterates by the thousands – and on the rate-payers' money. People like us are jolly fortunate in being able to afford to opt out. It's obviously worth it, even though the expense *is* a bind.'

Edith sincerely hoped that it was worth it because Edward often described Felicity's fees in more dramatic terms: 'ruinous' was the word he favoured. It must be nice to be able to dismiss such expenditure with a joky word like 'bind'.

'What a lovely chat we've had! We really must do it more often, Edith my dear, but now I simply must fly! I've got some people coming for dinner, not friends you know, just boring business. But I'm giving them steak and asparagus so that's no hassle – Brown's have some lovely asparagus in, you should get some – but it's the sweet that is a bit tricky. I'm doing something rather dramatic. . . .'

Instead of flying, Miranda launched into cookery chat. She never gives up, thought Edith. She guesses that I'm a rotten cook and is determined to interest me for my own good. No, she doesn't just guess, she *knows*; after all, she and Godfrey have been to dinner at Westwood from time to time.

'. . . the great thing is to add a dash of angostura to the egg whites after you whip them, and . . .'

Edith was nodding, her thoughts elsewhere. Now Miranda really could get a job if she wanted one, which is more than I could – even if I was free to take one. But it probably wouldn't be worth it for Miranda, 'tax-wise', as Godfrey would put it. Was Miranda really happy under all that bright chat? Spending her energies entertaining Godfrey's boring clients, getting into a great lather every year over the Conservative Association Garden Party – fairy-lights in the trees and dozens of quiches made over the weeks and stacked in the deep freeze; charting Jeremy's and Mary's progress through life – perhaps she kept diaries on Jeremy and Mary, à la Rose Kennedy! Edith smiled, involuntarily.

'Oh, I know what you're thinking,' Miranda had spotted the smile, 'that it'll all collapse when I turn it out! But it

34

shouldn't really, not if I get the gelatine just right and the cream firm enough. I'll tell you, anyway, how it goes and I'll copy the recipe out for you when I get a minute.'

'Lovely!' said Edith, trying not to think about the dismal menu that lay in wait for the family at Westwood.

Mrs Watson's car had gone from the drive by the time that Edith got home. She was pleased about that. Mrs Watson insisted on bringing her own vacuum cleaner with her to Westwood, declaring that Edith's was clapped out. Edith felt that the least she could do was to carry it out and stow it in the boot of Mrs Watson's car at the end of the morning's labour, and it was a task which she resented.

Samuel's freshly pressed suit hung in the kitchen, dark and gloomy like a carrion crow nailed to a post as a warning. There was a note lying on the table –

He was down for his elevens. Wants his lunch brought up on account of him being busy. Done my best with the suit but it won't take much more and the linings going. Can't budge that mark on the lapel. See you Thursday.

When Edith carried up his tray, she found Samuel in an expansive, jovial mood, the storm clouds of breakfast-time having seemingly quite blown away. It was thinking about his trip to London that had done it. His few remaining investments now seemed to be divided with care between such companies as held their shareholders' meetings in London and, preferably, those which also dispensed a few drinks and a platter or two of canapés on such occasions. There was, too, always the happy prospect of meeting an old chum who would invite him to a club for lunch. Samuel had long since ceased to be able to afford to keep up his own memberships. Friends from more affluent times were getting a bit thin on the ground (so many now being under it), but Samuel kept a weather eye open for the opportunity of cultivating new ones. Putting questions to the Board was stimulating and even more satisfying was the opportunity of giving them the benefit of his advice. Yes, Samuel looked forward to his little outings to the City.

'Mrs Watson's made a nice job of your suit. I think it's quite aired now, but I couldn't carry it along with the tray.'

'Don't worry, my dear. You can bring it up later. Can't think why you call that woman "Mrs Watson". It's not as though she's a housekeeper – God forbid! The woman must have a name – Annie or Jane, probably.' Samuel was pouring sherry from the decanter on his desk. He handed Edith a glass.

'Here, have a drink – why not, eh? Do you good, you look a bit peaky. Now what was I saying – yes, servants' names. Mother always called housemaids "Annie", said it saved trying to remember a whole string of names – there was always a bit of a turnover. It was the Fourteen-Eighteen that did it, y'know. Girls got paid too much for making munitions and never really settled down to domestic work after that. Munitions and all that Suffragette nonsense, that's what put the tin-hat on a decent standard of living. Got to be that you'd hardly get a girl for love or money!'

Edith stood sipping the sherry, which was rather dry for her taste, and doing her best to look interested. She'd heard it all before, oh so often. It would be hopeless to try to explain to Samuel that if she called Mrs Watson by her christian name then Mrs Watson would be quite likely to reciprocate and start addressing her as Edith – or even 'Edie'. Samuel had been having a pasting session again and had been wiping his sticky fingers on his jacket – Edith could tell, because his fingers were stuck all over with little bits of fluff.

'Too busy to get out to post these,' he was saying, pushing a pile of letters towards her. 'Just pop them in the box for me, will you. No rush, you can bring my suit up first. Just make sure they catch the afternoon collection.'

'I'll get them off right away,' said Edith, who had no intention of doing any such thing, but it was as good a pretext as any on which to make her escape.

2

Disturbed by the sudden chatter and clatter below, crows rose from the tree-tops, wheeling and cawing restlessly above their nests. Girls erupted from the side door of High Beeches, rushing in a tide of exuberance on to the wide lawns, golden green in the late afternoon sun. A trickle detached itself from the main flow as the day-girls made their way to the drive and freedom.

Felicity, after the initial headlong rush, paused at the first curve in the drive and craned her neck to gaze up at the birds. They always filled her with a strange unrest, fractionally this side of fear. Their dark shapes cut through the air, black crescents swooping and tumbling between the pale blue of the sky and the soft green haze of unfurling leaves.

'Come on!' Sally tugged on her arm. Sally never took notice of the crows; besides, she was impatient to get Felicity's attention. Sally had something exciting to tell her and had managed to hold it back all day until they would be alone together.

Other girls overtook them, in two and threes: the Juniors first, heads close, shrieking and giggling, swinging their satchels and breaking into coltish little runs. The Seniors who followed them walked purposefully, a little aloof, aware of their superiority.

The edges of the drive were delineated at intervals by grey stone toadstools. These, according to Miss Frobisher, had once been used to raise the floors of barns above the ground and thus prevent the entry of rats. Miss Frobisher was a mine of inconsequential information, and liberal with its imparting.

She prided herself that her girls, when eventually set loose upon the waiting world, would be able to hold their own in any conversation. Felicity dawdled along touching the top of every second toadstool, but briefly, almost furtively, in case Sally noticed and asked her why she did it. She couldn't have told her, because Felicity could not give an answer; she just knew, inside herself, that it would be prudent to do this and such inner convictions defied explanation.

The rest of the girls had already disappeared round the last bend in the drive; the noise of the boarders was distanced and the crows were settling down, flapping to roost on branches that creaked a little, still complaining with harsh, cross caws. Felicity had a habit of silence when in the company of more than one; now she felt ready to chatter. Sally recognised that her piece of news would have to wait.

'Grandfather was in a great wax at breakfast – another letter from old Lily Gudgeon!' She was peeling a small scab of lichen from a stone toadstool, it was the last of the series and she felt she should stand by it for a few seconds. 'The worst of it was that Grandfather had made a bish, he thought the letter was daft, but really it was pretty smart!'

'What did she say then?'

'Oh, the usual sort of thing – something about not getting out of her cottage. I don't think Grandfather will *ever* get her out!'

'But why should she get out if she doesn't want to?'

'So that Grandfather can make pots of money, silly!' Felicity gave an awkward little jump and changed step; they were outside the school grounds now, and she was being careful not to tread on the lines between the pavement slabs.

'I told you – if the building people could take down the cottage, then they'd be able to build a road through the end of our garden and put up lots of houses. Not just in the garden either, they'd be able to put houses in sort of terraces all down that slope at the side; you know, where the wood used to be, before it got cut down in the war. But the government, or someone, won't let Grandfather put a road in round there because of the motorway at the bottom; something to do with the traffic. Anyway, the only place the road can go is just where the cottage is – but old Lily won't budge. I wouldn't be surprised,' added Felicity, darkly, 'if Grandfather doesn't do something AWFUL to Lily Gudgeon if she goes on baiting him.'

'Like what?'

'Oh you know, setting fire to the cottage; sending her chocolates with poison in them. Something like that!' But Felicity's voice lacked conviction. Grandfather *said* a great deal but he never actually *did* very much.

'Mummy says that your grandfather is a reactionary old Fascist!'

'What's that mean?' asked Felicity, genuinely interested and impressed, as always, by Sally's command of important-sounding words.

'Well, you know . . . someone like your grandfather.'

'Horrible?'

'Yes, I suppose so. Mummy says that even the Tories won't have him – that's why they kicked him out of their Committee!'

'They did not then!' Felicity sounded indignant, her proprietorial instinct having been aroused. Grandfather might be pretty beastly, but he was hers, after all, to malign or protect, not Sally Pewter's.

'He resigned. He said he had more important things to do than chew the rag with a lot of dithering old poops who don't know their arse from their elbow. That's what HE said,' she added defiantly, seeing Sally's eyes grow round with shock. Grandfather's utterances often had that effect which which was the reason for Felicity's diligence in memorising them.

'That's rude!' said Sally, virtuously. She'd had enough of Felicity's grandfather, it was high time to drop her own bombshell.

'I'm leaving at the end of term – I'm telling you first, but I expect that everyone will know soon!' Sally may have had an inflated idea of the shock impact on the rest of the school, but Felicity's reaction was as amazed as she could have hoped. It had stopped her so suddenly in her tracks that she had stood right on a pavement crack and had had to put a hand out to the high brick wall for support. Felicity leaned against the wall now, her eyes wide, a branch of lilac had pushed her boater askew and the sweet, heavy scent of its blossoms filled her lungs as she took a quick intake of breath.

'Leaving?' Most of the extra air seemed to be expended on prolonging the first vowels so that the word shrieked out like a cry evoked by a sharp blow.

Sally nodded, a little disconcerted now by the intensity of Felicity's reaction. She began to wonder if her news was alarming, rather than exciting.

But Felicity's expression had swiftly changed to one of avid eagerness for more detail.

'I say, are you being kicked out? Did Frobisher find out about you cribbing in the history exam?'

'No, of course not!' Sally sounded indignant at the very suggestion that she should be found out, although, in fact, she usually was. Sally had little talent for hoodwinking authority and her attempts to do so were inspired more by envy of Felicity's amazing ability in that direction than by inclination.

'Well then, why ever *are* you leaving?'

'Because I'm starting at the Comprehensive at the end of the summer – that's why.'

'The Comprehensive?' The disbelief in Felicity's voice was undisguised. 'Go on, you're having me on, Sally Pewter!'

'No, I'm not . . . honest! Mummy says that I'll get a better education there – more relevant. They're awfully good on the Sciences, and Mummy says that's the field women should be breaking into. Even Granny says that High Beeches is a bit old hat nowadays. Miss Frobisher is out of touch.'

'But do you want to go to the Comprehensive – honestly?'

'It'll be all right.' Sally sounded a little defensive. 'No grotty old uniform any more. Mummy says that being free to

40

choose your own clothes develops your sense of individuality. Besides, private education is socially divisive . . . or something.'

Felicity brushed the lilac away from her shoulder. Sally's mother had something to say on anything and everything. Grandfather said that young Mrs Pewter was a fool and that being a child psychologist was all part and parcel of it. Any woman with a real concern for children would stay at home and look after her own, instead of gadding about to clinics that only wasted the rate-payers' money. He thought old Mrs Pewter, Sally's grandmother, was 'a rattling good sort' and thought it was hard cheese that she should be landed with such a ghastly daughter-in-law. Grandfather had gone on to say that daughters-in-law were not of one's own choosing and had to be borne with as much fortitude as one could muster. Mummy, Felicity had noticed, had said nothing to that but had put her hand up to her throat in that way she had – as though preventing a sound coming out; or perhaps she was imagining what it would be like to clutch her hand round Grandfather's fat mottled neck.

The girls were sauntering now, in silence. Felicity had pulled a piece of wall-cress from its cranny and was nipping the leaves off, one by one. She was tempted to tell Sally that she would miss her, miss her more than she felt inclined to admit even to herself. But she refrained: there was a smugness about Sally which should not be encouraged.

Sally broke the uncomfortable silence. 'We'll still see one another . . . weekends, holidays. Evenings too, if we don't get too much prep.' Felicity remained silent, so Sally continued, 'It won't make all that much difference, you'll see! Besides, I'll be able to tell you all about the Comprehensive – and the boys! Did you know that it's co-ed for most subjects?'

'Yes,' Felicity muttered. She hadn't known and didn't find the prospect as exciting as Sally seemed to, judging by the way her voice had taken on the light throw-away tone she used when she thought something to be really super.

They had reached the corner of the road where their ways

parted. 'You'll be coming round Saturday evening, won't you?'

Sally shook her head. 'Sorry, I can't. It's Mummy: she's having one of her Blacky parties, and I'll have to stay in to help with the handing-round and the washing-up. They always put her in a bad mood – she says it's the strain.'

'Why does she have them then?'

'Because we've got to make a multi-racial society work and it's up to the educated middle classes to set an example, that's why. The working classes are reactionary about colour, but it's not their fault, not really. It's to do with education. Do you know what "reactionary" means?'

Felicity had stopped listening, she was watching a solitary crow overhead. The bird seemed to falter, just above them and then flew off to circle over the trees in the direction of Westwood.

'Do you?' Sally persisted. Felicity shook her head.

'You should look it up then,' Sally advised. She intended to do so herself some day, but had not yet got round to it. 'You should always look up a word you don't understand. You can only put your point of view across if you have the right words, you know.'

'Your mother said that, too, did she?'

Sally coloured a little. There were times when she really hated Felicity Gordon-Fenn.

Her mother was in the kitchen when Felicity got in. She was browning the brisket in a pan on the top of the cooker, stabbing at it with a fork; it spat viciously, the flying sparks of fat sizzling on the burner and filling the air with blue, acrid smoke.

'Had a nice day, dear?' she asked in the tone of one who expected an answer no less conventionally inspired. But then she remembered that there was something which she wanted to ask Felicity. She gave the meat a bold jab and at last succeeding in rolling it over on its other side, above its threatening protest, she said – 'Felicity, I want you to spell "desiccated".'

Felicity, already eating the after-school snack left out for her on the kitchen table and wishing her mother wouldn't make banana sandwiches (they always turned into a brown soggy mush, slimy, yet strangely full of fibrous threads), mumbled 'Why?'

'Don't speak with your mouth full, and don't answer a question with a question, dear. Now, go on, spell it!'

'D-e-s-s-i-c-a-t-e-d. Can I take some more milk?'

'Yes – but it's "may", not "can".'

Edith heard the refrigerator door bang and Felicity's footsteps as she walked out of the kitchen, presumably taking her glass of milk with her. But she dared not turn round, not with the meat balanced so precariously between the fork and a spoon. Gingerly, her tongue nipped between her teeth, she lowered the charred meat on to its bed of carrots and onions in the deep pan of simmering water. Edith let out her held breath.

Fees, she thought crossly, fees, expensive uniform, music extra – but Felicity hadn't been taught how to spell! All very well for Edward to say that once Felicity got to university that would be the end of the expense. But, at this rate, would she pass her A Levels – everyone had to get those before entering upon that phase of education which freed one from the opportunity (or was it the obligation?) of paying for a private alternative. Still, she thought, banging the lid on the pan, Felicity *was* only twelve, and she was the quiet type; not at all a larking-about sort of a child. She'd settle down well enough to serious swotting when the time came – and there was quite a lot of time to go yet. Five or six years, in fact, she thought, suddenly appalled at the sum of money required to meet the fees for High Beeches over such a length of time. But the frightening thing is, she reflected, busy now chopping cabbage, that one cannot anticipate expenditure with certainty any more. Things keep going up relentlessly in cost – all very well for Miranda to ask for jumble, but dare one afford to throw *anything* away? Not knowing what trifle, unconsidered today, might cost the earth in a year's . . . six months' . . . time! She'd nearly forgotten – she walked to the door and called out to Felicity who appeared, reluctantly, at the morning-room door.

'I'm just watching telly!'

'There's something I want you to do first. Won't take a minute.' Edith beckoned Felicity to the kitchen (Samuel might appear in the hall and witness the transaction), and handed her the letters which she had kept in a drawer. 'Pop these in the post, would you? Grandfather believes that I posted them at lunchtime – so not a word!'

Edith was gratified that Felicity, instead of arguing or pouting as a less agreeable child might have done, smiled as she took the bundle. Felicity's smiles were of a particular quality, both grave and sweet in their nature and born, apparently, only after consideration; nor did her smile stop at lips and teeth, but it extended to the whole face, giving it warmth and light. They were rare, Felicity's smiles, not carelessly thrown around or randomly given, but kindly bestowed.

Felicity scampered down the drive but, once out of sight of the house, she turned off into the shrubbery. Crouching, she tunnelled through the bushes until she reached a favourite hidy-hole under a rhododendron ancient enough to have grown spindly so that one could sit quite comfortably under its cover. She skiffed through the envelopes. Three were addressed to editors of national papers, one to the local paper, one to a Government Minister and another to the Race Relations Board. These she opened, carefully slitting the lower edge with a hair-slide, extracted the contents and then tore off the top corner of the envelope – stamp intact. Six twelvepenny stamps. 'Not bad!' she whispered, folding them in her handkerchief. A boarder would gladly buy them for fifty or sixty pence. She tore up the letters and mutilated envelopes and thrust them down a hole at the root of the rhododendron. Felicity wondered what lived down that hole, because the shredded correspondence which she frequently put down it always seemed to disappear. Perhaps some houseproud little mouse lovingly lined a snug nursery with it at the end of the tunnel : floor and walls pale blue, decorated with the darker blue squiggles of Grandfather's bold handwriting! Felicity giggled. At least, thanks to her, some of Grandfather's labours served a useful purpose!

The remaining letter was addressed to the local Member of Parliament and that, regretfully, was best left intact. Grandfather had once stormed along to the MP's 'Surgery' and complained bitterly about receiving no reply to a letter. Eventually the inefficiency of the postal service was held responsible and it had proved to be an ill wind from which Felicity had derived quite a profit in the shape of stamps from several envelopes addressed to that institution. But she had decided that it was wiser, on the whole, not to tamper with letters to the MP and these now enjoyed the same immunity as she accorded to missiles addressed to the bank and to those of a clearly private nature.

Felicity remained for some little time under the bush, enjoying the sweet sense of concealment in the cool, green dimness where the sunshine did not penetrate.

3

Dinner was a rather silent meal. The circumstance of the meat being tough was a contributory factor, requiring, as it did, concentrated, dedicated chewing. Samuel remarked on its shortcomings, but only briefly. At intervals he busied himself with the little silver toothpick which he kept in his waistcoat pocket. Excavating between his strong yellow molars, he congratulated himself yet again on his good fortune in retaining his own teeth; God only knew how he could have coped with Edith's cooking if he had been reduced to dentures. He would have remarked on that, too, but for the physical impossibility of plying the toothpick and talking at one and the same time.

The arrival of the sago pudding lessened the strain, although it did little to stimulate the digestive juices.

'Sally's leaving High Beeches. She's going to the Comprehensive after the summer hols,' Felicity said, in the hope that this piece of information would arrest her mother's hand which seemed about to plunge the spoon into the glutinous mass to deliver another helping to Felicity's plate.

'Good gracious!' Edith dropped the spoon back in the serving dish, where it bounced a little on impact with the pudding.

'I did hear that young Mrs Pewter is going to stand as a Labour candidate at the local Council Elections. I thought it was only a rumour, but it would seem that it must be true – judging from such a move!' said Edward with a little, pinched smile.

'Good God!' Samuel was shaking his head, but more in sorrow than in anger. 'Poor old Kate Pewter – what a thing, eh? A viper like that in the bosom of the family! Who'd be a parent – not knowing what your children may drag home. Mind you, Kate was always a bit too easy-going – I could have told her. First time I clapped eyes on young Tom's intended, I said to myself, "There's trouble, if you like!" I can always read a character pretty shrewdly. It's the little things that give people away, y'know. That sort of girl, degree of some sort, big feet, untidy hair, opinionated and never out of trousers – you could tell right away how it would turn out. Poor Kate!' Samuel pushed his pudding plate away as though his appetite had quite vanished.

Edith made the mistake of asking, 'Aren't you hungry?'
'Well, perhaps I could just manage a bit of cheese to finish off,' was Samuel's reply and she had to go and fetch what she had had no intention of serving.

Felicity was not expected to help with the washing-up on weekdays during term. She had her own study upstairs, but only occupied it briefly, spending as short a time as possible there; just sufficient time to leave an impression that the room was used for the purpose intended. An old textbook, changed from time to time, left on the desk; a few sheets of paper in disarray, a toffee wrapper or two and a screw of paper thrown in the wastepaper basket, these provided the illusion of usage. The room had once been her bedroom, but she had persuaded her mother to permit her to sleep, instead, in a room at the top of the house, reached by way of the kitchen stairs and designed originally to hold the beds of two or three maids. To wish to sleep up there, so removed from the rest of the household and in such a bleak room, had seemed a strange request and one which Edith would not have granted had Felicity's declared reason not seemed such a reasonable one. Felicity had told her mother that the movements made by the family below, the noise on the stairs and in the corridor as they went to bed, disturbed her. Edith was aware that Felicity frequently wakened during the night, and she had often discovered her wide awake when she had chanced to slip in to see her on her own way to bed. Once Felicity's wish had been granted and her bed had been moved up to the room so remote from the rest of the family, she had set about making the room more attractive than one would have thought possible. Edith, feeling a little guilty that Felicity should be forced to sleep in such an unlikely room in order to be undisturbed, had felt unable to deny her the acquisition of such pieces of furniture, rugs, cushions and even ornaments and pictures which she coveted from other rooms in Westwood.

Felicity continued to lie awake at times in the night, but had not expected it to be otherwise, as she was quite aware that these awakenings had never had anything whatsoever to do with her sleep being interrupted by noise; it was simply the way she was made and she accepted the fact without resentment. Edith was unaware that Felicity's habit of broken sleep remained unaltered as she never climbed to her daughter's room in the night in case the noise of her approach awakened her.

Despite the fact that her old room had been converted into a study, Felicity preferred to do her prep in the bedroom that was now so snug. There, she could concentrate in a way that was impossible for her in any other part of Westwood where she felt in some mysterious way diminished, less herself and more a part of something, both past and present, from which she would rather stand apart. Sometimes, lying briefly awake in the dark but not at all afraid of her isolation, she thought that the room suited her so well because it had never been occupied by Gordon-Fenns. This room had remained apart, the refuge of long-gone maids who had been free to leave Westwood and the Gordon-Fenns whenever the mood took them.

Edith was comfortably settled for the evening in what was still called the 'morning-room' but which could now more correctly be described as an all-purpose living-room. She had turned the television on but was not actually watching it; its sound, however, was companionable. Edith was inclined to think that the television set provided the best sort of company, company which required no voiced response, no personal service and which could be dismissed at the touch of a button. She was busy darning the elbows of one of Edward's cardigans. Edward himself was shut away in his study, working, or so he said. Felicity would join her mother presently, and together, without obligation to chat, they could watch the nature programme which would soon be coming on. Samuel was upstairs, presumably watching his own television set. Edith was truly thankful that he had at length been persuaded to buy his own set. Samuel had capitulated only after a terrible row. Nothing ever seemed to be changed at Westwood without argument and as Edith and Edward both disliked rows and open hostility, the result was that differences of opinion were rarely resolved and overt tension went unrelieved. It had been Samuel's phase as a champion of Mary Whitehouse that had brought matters to a head. Night after night during those terrible months they had been condemned to sit through all sorts of disagreeable and tasteless programmes which they would never normally have dreamed of watching. It had been so bad for Felicity. Samuel, crouched over a clip-board, had argued that his compilation of complaints had been in the interests of Felicity and all the other young and innocent children who were being subjected to exposure to such filth. Edith, however, had been unable to agree that it could possibly be in Felicity's interest that she should be repeatedly dismissed to her own room when she might have been happily watching an Underwater World of Wonder or some such innocent programme on the other channel.

But in the end it had all turned out for the best. Samuel had been forced to give in and buy his own set and now, although his moral-watchdog phase had waned, he had mercifully got into the habit of viewing in the privacy of his own room. Edith was pleased to reflect that sometimes things did turn out well and that even the longest lane had a turning; no, she corrected herself, squinting a little as she re-threaded her needle, that was not quite right! It was a long lane that

49

had *no* turning – that was it. Well, one must just trust and pray that one's feet were not placed on a lane of that order! When Lily Gudgeon died – and it must be 'when' and not 'if': after all, death came to everyone in the end, even the Samuels and Lily Gudgeons of this world (although one could appreciate the Almighty's reluctance to gather them in); *when* Lily died and the cottage became vacant, then Samuel's affairs (and, by association, those of Edward) would definitely take an upturn. Edith recognised that it would not all be unalloyed joy. She did not look forward to the grounds of Westwood being filled with houses, other people's children, barking dogs and cars with doors to be slammed. None of that would really worry Samuel as long as he could finish his life in Westwood with some money to spare. Even if Lily should outlive Samuel, Edith was sure that she, Felicity and Edward would still be imprisoned in this tomb of lost aspirations as Edward would certainly not sell Westwood until he had made a profit out of the development of its land; in that respect Edward was as stubborn and obsessional as his father. In Lily Gudgeon they had met their match. Wretched woman, no wonder Samuel hates her so! Edith checked her thoughts. It was bad enough, she told herself, to muddle on from day to day keeping up an ineffectual charade of a life style for which the rest of society seemed to have nothing but contempt, without allowing her mind to become poisoned with thoughts about the need for the death of those who stood in the way of one's freedom.

Edith had ceased to sew and sat, hands motionless on the work on her lap, gazing unseeingly at the television screen where a badger was contentedly scratching the fleas from his flanks.

Felicity came silently in and sat quietly in an armchair facing the set. She left it on when, the programme over, she got up to prepare her own and her grandfather's bedtime cocoa. At some point during the programme, Edith had fallen asleep and Felicity knew that to switch off the set might be to awaken her.

Samuel came down to the kitchen to fetch his cocoa, not from any sudden generosity of spirit but because he wanted to find someone to listen to the questions which he proposed to put to the Board of Universal Toiletries.

'Where's your mother, then?' He was peering round the kitchen as though Edith might be discovered lurking in some ill-lit recess.

'She was watching the telly and now she's dropped off.' Felicity had taken the milk from the refrigerator and its door hung open. Samuel, drawn by the harsh oblong of light, was now poking about searching for the remains of the Edam.

'Dropped off . . . dropped out! That's the epitaph of the new generation!' he grumbled. The refrigerator rocked a little on the uneven floor under the pressure of his weight as he hauled himself upright. Ham stock slopped from an over-filled bowl into a dish of tinned peaches on the shelf below, thus enhancing Edith's reputation as a provider of unique fare.

Samuel peeled the wax rind from the cheese and let it fall to the floor where it would subsequently cling and do nothing to improve Mrs Watson's temper.

'We should be holding on – not dropping off and dropping out!'

'Mummy's tired.' Felicity passed him his mug of cocoa and primly added a plate for his cheese and biscuits.

Samuel opened his mouth to say more but then, changing his mind, stuffed it with cheese instead. No good wasting words on a child too young, or too stupid, to grasp the wider implications of his exhortation. Pity, though, he would have liked to have told someone – anyone – about how he was going to shake the complacency of the Board tomorrow. 'Had they,' he would put it to them, 'had they made contingency plans to exploit to the full the development of the silicon chip?' Properly exploited, it could mean the halving of the work force and the doubling of dividends. Fewer jobs, increased unemployment, that would bring the unions to heel – and not before time! Some straight talking, that's what the Board needed to ginger them up; make them realise that some shareholders took an intelligent interest in scientific development and its implications and were not prepared to be fobbed off with vague assurances!

'Holding on is only part of it! One has to thrust forward, consolidate, meet shop-floor militancy with resolution. The voice of authority must ring out!'

Samuel suddenly realised that he was waving a biscuit and jabbing his knife at a deserted kitchen. Felicity had gone: unobtrusively, in that silent way of hers, and taking her cocoa with her. The cat was yowling at the back door. Well, let it yowl, thought Samuel. That cat did nothing to justify its existence. Never once had it been seen to actually catch a mouse – it was too busy shedding hair on the furniture, ripping the moquette when it was alone and stealing food when one's back was turned. Useless eunuch! Samuel gave the back door a resounding kick and, limping slightly, made his way upstairs where he would pour himself a generous tot of whisky, the last of the day, which he described to himself as 'the tassel on the night-cap'.

The lilac flopped sickly in its vase, shedding brown, brittle blossoms on the table. Felicity absent-mindedly gathered them together in a heap with a finger that left gleaming trails on the dusty rosewood.

The landing and the corridor were dimly lit, a low-wattage bulb being left on all night in case Samuel needed to go to the lavatory. He frequently experienced such a need, but as he preferred to use the Kilner jar which he kept for that purpose in his bedside locker, there was little danger of Felicity's presence being discovered: it never was. Her ears were finely tuned to noise, not only to the rattle of a door-knob, the sound of a footfall, but to a myriad of subtle, scarcely audible sounds; the dry rubbing as the velvet folds of the landing window curtains moved in the air that ever so faintly rattled the glass as it insinuated itself round the window-panes; the slight whistle of a draught that blew under a door, rustling a fallen lilac leaf on the floor and chilling her feet; the creak of floorboards gently shifting where no foot fell. The wail of despair that seeped from the walls, lost itself in the darkness but left a wave of movement in the air that pressed against her eardrums. She could smell things, too: the odour of ammonia that rose from the faded patches on the carpet, silent witness to the incontinent habits of Edwina's long dead sealyham, whining in the chill, lonely draught while his mistress slept too deeply to hear, or lay awake too unsteady to heed; stale pipe-tobacco smoke; the scent of the dying lilac; dust; a tang of sap as she raised a hand to nibble at her thumb joint; and, under all that, the sour whiff of ancient regrets and despairs that assailed her through her pores rather than her nostrils.

Felicity moved quietly towards the head of the stairs. She stood for a moment staring down at the darkness below, her hand raised, her tongue nipped between her teeth in the manner of a snake testing the air. She moved away, down the corridor. At the door of Samuel's office she stopped and entered the room. She could hear Samuel's bubbling snores from the adjoining room but she took the precaution of quietly closing the connecting door before letting the beam of her torch sweep the office. The paperweights gleamed like watching eyes in the path of the light. Grandfather had told her that they would be left to her when he died. She caressed one now, cupping her hand over its cool rotundity. Samuel's gun glinted in its usual place in the window embrasure. Something rustled in the wastepaper basket, Felicity switched off her torch, crept closer and suddenly switched it on again, pointing it downwards and bringing sudden shocked stillness to the mouse that stared up at her from the bottom of an empty biscuit packet whose smooth waxed sides afforded no hold for scrabbling paws.

Felicity unscrewed the top from Samuel's tobacco jar and then, pinching the mouth of the packet together, she lifted it from the wastepaper basket and decanted its surprised captive into the half-empty jar. She screwed the lid swiftly back in place. The little chip in the lip of the jar would allow the mouse sufficient air to keep him in lively fettle until Grandfather needed to fill his pipe in the morning.

On her way back along the corridor, Felicity paused briefly outside her parents' room. Her ear to the door, she could just hear their breathing and, in her mind's eye, saw them, back to back, dreaming the last hours of the night away.

Her back to the door which gave access to the servants' stairs, she stood for a moment looking down the long corridor. She did not know what it was that she sought on these silent prowlings in the night. Like a tongue irresistibly drawn to prod at a sensitive tooth, her feet carried her in the stillness of the dark stealthily through the house. She thrust open the knobless door and it swung shut behind her with a puff of air and the whisper of felt on felt.

She ran coltishly up the uncarpeted stairs, the light from her open bedroom door flowing to meet her, the torch in her dressing-gown pocket bumping against her thigh and knew, now, that she would sleep undisturbed until morning. It was safe, now, to smile and, thinking about the mouse, she did. She would tell Sally about it when they were alone – or perhaps she wouldn't; a secret was more fun when it really was a secret unshared.

4

The answer, Edith told herself, might lie in vitamins; she ought to get some from the chemist's . . . c, or was it b? She'd switched to buying bread of the wholemeal kind, but it hadn't seemed to have made much difference — except to Samuel who complained that it gave him indigestion. Samuel had appeared rather odd at breakfast time, abstracted. Perhaps he'd only been thinking about the day ahead in London. It looked as though he had cut himself in shaving, at least there had been blood on his chin; but the sticking plaster had been on his thumb, very odd.

She really shouldn't feel as exhausted as she did; tired, naturally, because although it was not yet lunchtime she had already done a great deal of work. But this aching weariness that made her feel she would never be capable of rising from the armchair into which she had flung herself, surely that was not quite normal?

Edith, after cleaning Samuel's rooms (tobacco had been strewn all over the carpet in his office, quite disgusting), had gone into the drawing-room to fling wide the windows and allow the sun and air to dispel the musty, damp odour of disuse that clung to the room. This would require to be done daily before the Bring and Buy a week hence, if it was not to be apparent to her guests that this room was rarely used.

It is not as though I am really middle-aged, she assured herself. Well, perhaps early-middle-aged, she conceded. Forty-five was regarded almost as a woman's prime nowadays. Look at the Queen . . . Mrs Thatcher! Both older than me, she thought, rubbing her arm where the corner of one of Samuel's metal filing cabinets had bruised it. *They* seem full of energy. That woman on the wireless (the one who had chirped about the importance of vitamins), she had recommended honey too, and a full sex life. She could certainly do something about the honey. There was no point in going to see Dr Carey, it was not as though she could claim terrible *symptoms*. She could only rabbit on about never really wanting to get up in the morning, having to force herself through the day's chores, often feeling that she was trapped in a forest – the light dim and the terrain so flat and the trunks of the trees so tall that she would never see where the forest ended; assuming it ever did. But just to know that a clearing or two lay ahead would be a comfort! A clearing where the sunshine penetrated and where she could bask for a little without anyone in sight, certainly no Samuel, Edward or Felicity. No, to pour all that into Dr Carey's ear was unthinkable. Besides, according to Miranda, whatever ailed a woman after the age of forty, doctors breezily dismissed as being due to the onset of the menopause and fobbed one off with tranquillisers and a bracing chat.

Edith was staring at the marble fireplace: it was white but faintly streaked with greenish black like an underripe Gorgonzola. It always put her in mind of a sepulchre and the black papier-mâché tray, with its faded garland of flowers which acted as a firescreen, heightened the illusion. It would have been a happier choice to have sat in a chair facing the open french window, the fresh breeze might even be enjoyable if it was directed at her face and not coming at her from behind. But she really couldn't summon up the energy to move, not, at any rate, for a few minutes.

It was a very unsatisfactory sort of a room, Edith told herself, letting her eyes roam – that, at least, was not too exhausting. A hotch-potch of a room, she decided. Yet the basic proportions were good, one could – with money – achieve something rather elegant with such a room. The only one who had approached its furnishing with the advantage of money had been Samuel's mother, Dora, but she had been patently short on taste. The dark Turkey carpet, the heavy Victorian mahogany, the concert Broadwood with its obscenely fat legs and grinning keys like stained dentures, all that had been Dora. The white bearskin in front of the fireplace, the little Tiffany table lamp (only 'Tiffany type', Edith amended, if it had been genuine then Samuel would most likely have sold it by now), the frivolous little ornaments scattered here and there like a charm bracelet on a glowering dowager, these must have been Edwina's contribution. They were relics, no doubt, of Edwina's and Samuel's palmy days when they had lived in a smart London flat. They looked all wrong, these little bits and pieces juxtaposed with Dora's Indian ornaments. Ganesa, the Elephant God, stood on the mantelpiece; carved in black ebony, bizarre, even menacing with its trunk and tusks but face and hands which were human. Ganesa, in fact, was endowed with four hands and that, thought Edith sourly, was appropriate equipment for domestic life in Westwood.

The only mark that Edith had herself made on the room was in the provision of a new set of loose covers, and that had been out of necessity. Even they, she noted, looked as though they could do with a cleaning, the bearskin had a dingy look, too. She suspected that soot gusted down the unused chimney in the winter gales: there was always a hint of its sharp, sour smell on the still air when the windows were closed.

James and Dora Fenn stared down at her from their respective wide gilt frames on either side of the mantelpiece. They had been just plain 'Fenn' originally, it had been Dora who had introduced her own surname. One could tell, just by looking at her, that she must have longed to sneak in a hyphen; Edith suspected that it must have been James who had thwarted that ambition – he looked like a man who would have regarded the acquisition of a hyphen with amused contempt. It had been Samuel, unhampered by any sense of social propriety, who had introduced the hyphen to the family surname after the death of his father. Samuel was proud of the portraits which had been commissioned by

Dora when she and James had retired from India to live out the rest of their lives in Westwood. Samuel declared that the portraits gave 'a certain air' to the drawing-room. They certainly did that. One could see the resemblance between Samuel and his father in the heavy features, thick neck and blue eyes; but James Fenn's eyes were deep-set and shrewd, with no trace of the bulbous goggle of those of his son.

Dora, her husband's junior by quite twenty years, did not look it. But India had been cruel to white women, ravaging their skin and, or so it appeared in Dora's case, souring their natures. But perhaps it was unjust to place all the blame upon the climate of India – Dora looked like a woman in whom the milk of human kindness would have curdled early irrespective of where she had lived. No, thought Edith, I am being uncharitable. From what Edith had learned of the family history, it was clear that poor Dora had had more than her share of misfortune. Just thinking about Dora's life made Edith feel a little ashamed of her own discontents. Dora had been born into the higher echelons of Indian Civil Service life but, shortly after her return to India from school in England, both her parents had died of cholera. Dora had been given a home by friends of her parents but their own pretty and vivacious daughters had quite over-shadowed the plain and dumpy Dora and they had success-fully captured the more eligible men who had swum into the orbit of their family. At twenty-five, painfully conscious of her invidious position and perhaps suspecting that her adoptive family were beginning to regard her as a tiresome spinster embarrassment, Dora had settled for marriage to James Fenn. James, already in his mid-forties, could have had little to recommend him to a young woman beyond his bachelorhood and his undoubted financial success. A stout and earthy Calcutta jute merchant fitted uneasily into the socially superior milieu in which Dora had been accustomed to move. In fact he did not fit at all, and gradually the Fenns had found themselves in some social isolation – Dora refusing to mix with what, in her opinion, was an undesirable boxwallah circle. But although she had refused the embrace of his world, Dora did dutifully accept that of James himself and suffered a succession of miscarriages as a result. When, eventually, young Samuel was born and showed every sign of surviving (one could imagine Samuel as having been no less than a lusty baby), Dora had badgered James into retiral to England in his early fifties, an earlier age than a man of such financial vigour would have wished.

It would have been strange if Samuel had not been indulged and spoiled. When James had died, Samuel had been only eighteen and Dora had had him all to herself. It couldn't have been easy, Edith conceded, gazing at Dora, living with such a woman, trying to fulfil her expectations and striving to withstand her domination. Stout, indomitable Dora, staring from the canvas with wintry grey eyes and straight little mouth pursed between pendulous cheeks, could scarcely have been an agreeable influence. But possibly the artist had been less than generous to his sitter – Dora had the look of a woman who might well have haggled over the fee.

Edwina had never been painted in oils, or, if she had, no evidence of the fact survived. But there was a tinted photographic portrait of her in the drawing-room. Edith, a little restored, walked to the piano where it stood and took the silver-framed photograph in her hands. She wiped the dust from the glass with the cloth she had been using in Samuel's room and a little flurry of biscuit crumbs and tobacco pattered on to the carpet. Edwina had been more than pretty, but not quite beautiful – the mouth was a trifle too full and slack for that. There was a vivacious eagerness about Edwina's expression, bordering on the hectic. Edith examined the face carefully, tilting the photograph this way and that, almost as though she was studying the portrait of a woman whom she had never seen. But she had; she had seen Edwina in the last years of her life, but by then very little trace of this early, youthful Edwina had remained. Well, thought Edith judiciously, one could see the similarity, for instance there was the fine bone structure – time had never altered that, had brought it to the fore if anything; there was the delicate line of the chin – an asset in a woman, but an unfortunate feature for her son, Edward, to have inherited. There was no doubt that Felicity had inherited quite a lot of her paternal grandmother's looks, but the resemblance was elusive. Taken one by one, the similarity in each component part was apparent, but the overall effect was indefinably different. It was the sparkle, Edith decided with clinical detachment, that was missing in Felicity. Felicity's face conveyed a sense of gravity, secretiveness, perhaps. Or was it withdrawal? But, God knows, thought Edith, frowning at the recollection, poor Edwina's expression in her latter years had been starkly withdrawn.

Edward could not have been much older than seven when Edwina and Samuel had had to sell up and make their home with Dora. Such an impressionable age for a child! Edith found the ready tears of over-tiredness flooding her eyes as she imagined what that household must have been like. Dora, who from all accounts had detested Edwina, venting her spite and resentment without let or hindrance from the strength of her position as their financial provider. Samuel, smarting from his business disaster (which he must have realised was due entirely to his own ineptitude and folly compounded by Edwina's extravagance and frivolity), roaring about like a wounded bear. Things must have been a little better after Dora's death three years later, but even these three years must have left an ineradicable mark on Edward. What came after, as far as Edith could gather, had not been that much of an improvement.

Little of what Edith had pieced together of the Gordon-Fenn family saga had been learned from either Samuel or Edward, neither of whom were inclined to discuss the past in any coherent detail. Most of what Edith knew had been told to her by old Kate Pewter, Sally's grandmother. Kate was a contemporary of Samuel's and perhaps, before Kate had married, Dora had had designs on her as an acceptable daughter-in-law. It had been Kate's father who had been persuaded by Dora to find the young Samuel a place in the world of commodity broking. That was how the seeds of disaster had been so lightly sown.

No, Edith protested to herself, wiping the back of a hand roughly across her eyes and banging Edwina's photograph back on to the piano, I will *not* waste my sympathy on any of you! 'Least of all on you!' she said aloud to the chill room, glaring at Dora's portrait. 'Perhaps you did have a rotten life, but you most likely asked for it – fat, pompous, aristo-cratic, domineering, bitter old woman that you were! I bet,' she went on, moving closer to the fireplace from where the painting looked even uglier, 'I bet you loved being a mem-sahib, queening it over a bungalow full of servants! Despis-ing your husband but not being too proud to grab his money. You,' she said, giving the frame a rap with her fist, 'you were nothing but a disageeable old cow – so there!'

Perhaps it had been the angle at which she had been holding her head, craning upwards as she looked up those haughty nostrils, but something had made Edith feel quite dizzy and not a little foolish, screeching in that childish and vulgar way at a dingy painting. She held on to the mantelpiece with both hands for a minute, her head bowed and resting against the deathly cold marble. Her body felt like a cord stretched between hands and feet and, like a string held taught, it trembled and soon she was shivering with a violence which even the coldness of the room scarcely warranted. In less than a minute it was over and, feeling strangely relaxed and calm, she pushed herself away from the mantelpiece. Edith had experienced it before, this sudden paroxysm of rage which swept like a storm through her body, spent itself and receded, leaving her with an illusion of being purged of resent-ment. But it was only an illusion, a temporary respite until the pressure built up again.

Edith stooped and, with a hand that scarcely trembled, retrieved the duster which she had earlier flung to the floor. She was conscious of gratitude for these occasional and merci-fully private explosions. It was implosion that she feared.

5

Her mother had taken the key to the attic door from the board which hung in the disused laundry-room and given it and a black plastic bag to Felicity with a diffident request that Felicity should have a search in the attic for anything suitable for Miranda's jumble sale.

Edith need not have felt apologetic. Felicity was enjoying herself poking about in the attic, it was a better way than most to spend a wet Saturday afternoon.

The rain sounded heavier, up here under the eaves, drumming on the slates and gurgling down the gutters. Felicity had taken Puss-puss with her and now, resentful at being hauled from his place by the morning-room fire, he glared at her from the nest he had trodden in a pile of mildewed dust-sheets.

The naked light, swinging gently in the currents of air that gusted under the roof, scarcely penetrated the crepuscular gloom of the far corners of the attic, but in the beam of her torch Felicity could see the bats which had so terrified her mother. They hung like a cluster of dried leaves from a beam at the far end of the attic. She considered poking them with a broom handle to see how Puss-puss would react to the sight of flying mice, but decided against it. One of Miss Frobisher's titbits of information for conversational use had been that bats never entangled themselves in human hair, but then one could not be altogether sure that Miss Frobisher was infallible. Besides, the attic smelt decidedly rancid in the vicinity of the bats. Felicity weaved her way through the piles of junk towards the area which lay within the pool of light. According to her mother, there should be a tin cabin trunk somewhere which was filled with old-fashioned household linen.

She spotted it, under a pile of worm-eaten deckchair frames. The harvest of years of Dora's labours lay within. Crocheted doilies, antimacassars, table runners in drawn threadwork, wool-embroidered cushion covers in crash linen, handkerchief sachets, tatted table mats, dressing-table sets in écru and coffee-coloured thread; Felicity dragged them out by the handful and stuffed them in the plastic sack. They had been crammed, higgledy-piggledy, into the trunk with no greater respect than Felicity now afforded them.

Just when it seemed that the plastic sack could not hold any more, Felicity was relieved to come upon a layer of tissue paper which she at first assumed lined the bottom of the trunk. But it gave, spongily, under her hand. Below it lay dresses which had been folded with such evident care that Felicity found herself handling them gently; not shaking them from their folds or lifting them clear of the tissue paper, but running her hands sensuously over the fabric. Shot silk slithered under her fingers, the colours iridescent and shimmering like petrol on water, tussore, crêpe de Chine and chiffon gently arrested the glide of her fingers with their soft-textured surface. She found herself holding her breath, strangely excited as she peeled back the corner of each layer of paper, almost stealthily, sliding her hands under the folds. Scent rose from the disturbed material, stale and musty but not unpleasant. Her fingers found the edge of a box and she drew it out slowly, pulling it sideways and upwards so as not to disturb what had been laid with such care on top of it. It was a large chocolate box, its lid a riot of painted roses, a wide bow of apricot pink satin was fixed astride one corner. The box was surprisingly heavy. The lid lifted off with a faint sucking noise, as though the air of the attic rushed into a long dead vacuum. It was crammed with beads, glass, imitation pearl, coral, paste; long strings that Felicity threaded over a wrist so that the multi-coloured strands cascaded down to the bottom of the trunk, winking and glinting in the light, clinking and tinkling faintly as they swayed one against the other. There was something else in the box, a long slim ivory tube banded with jade and flattened at one end into what she at last recognised as a mouthpiece.

A shot rang out almost below her feet. Puss-puss leaped from his watching place and streaked across the attic to the half-open door. Felicity was jerked abruptly back into the present, but was not unduly startled. She knew that it was only Grandfather taking pot-shots from his window at a magpie or a pigeon.

The rain had eased, there was now only a gentle pattering on the slates. Felicity felt chilled and her knees were uncomfortable on the gritty, rough boards. She wondered for how long she had been crouched there, mesmerised, lost in a world which she had never known, touched by hints of memories which were not her own. Her mother would be wondering what she was up to – might perhaps climb the stairs to discover what it was that was delaying her. Felicity let the beads slide from her arm back into the box and then, on impulse, hastily snatched up a few strings and the cigarette-holder before replacing the lid. She stuffed the beads into the front of her blouse and they lay heavy against her warm skin.

She understood what it was that she had so unexpectedly found and who it was who had so carefully laid these things away as though, by their preservation, a certain period of time would be prevented from vanishing. It was Edwina's heyday that had been so gently laid to rest; the days of her grandmother's youth which had been made gay and lively by the possession of money. The salad days which had ended when the money had run out and it could only have been Edwina herself who had taken such pains to preserve their memory. Felicity replaced the sheets of tissue paper, smoothing them almost reverently. It was hard to imagine her grandfather as having been part of such enchanted days – but perhaps he had started off as a prince and it was the lack of money that had changed him into a horrible toad. Money, thought Felicity, her hands momentarily arrested in their caressing glide by the sheer brilliance of her sudden flash of insight, money and magic were almost the same thing! Money could change things, make wishes come true. No wonder the grown-ups were always on about it – its acquisition or its lack. But they made it sound boring, as though its only function was for dreary things like paying bills for things which one really needed.

The tissue paper looked so neat, so clean, it was an invitation to lift, to pry, to see what lay concealed beneath. Felicity looked around and saw a pile of old *Tatlers*. Discarding the top copy which was grey with dust, she lifted a handful of the magazines and strewed them over the paper. As she twisted sideways to reach for a few more copies, the clump of necklaces under her blouse loosened a little and the beads shifted and stirred stealthily against her flesh. She found the sensation not unpleasant. It felt as though she had taken to her a small, cold little animal and now, no longer moribund, it basked gratefully in the heat of her body, tickling her skin as it twitched with the tentative movements of life restored.

6

His shot had missed. The magpie had flown away unscathed, launching itself slowly into the air; almost insolently, or so it seemed to Samuel.

The light was bad, the sky heavy with low, sullen cloud. It was no wonder, Samuel told himself, that he had miffed the shot. He stood a little longer at the open window, the gun slack in his hands, the wind gusting in his face, spattering him with droplets of water from the tendrils of ivy that drooped above the window. He hauled on the window which juddered sluggishly in its warped frame and then finished the course with an alarming rush of speed to close with a bang that rattled the panes.

Papers had blown from his desk and lay on the floor, stirring slightly in the draught that blew under the door that led to his adjoining bedroom. He let them lie, reluctant to stoop for fear of disturbing whatever it was that lurked in the region of his stomach. It was all very well for Dr Carey to dismiss it as 'merely a touch of wind'. To Samuel it possessed a solidity, a shape, ill-defined but actual for all that. He seized a pile of old company reports and tapped them into a neat block, noisily, rapping them hard on the desk to drown the whispered words that rose to the surface of his mind – 'a growth'. No one told one anything nowadays – at least not directly. One had to read between the lines, tap one's way along like a blind man, senses strained to pick up nuances; detect the dangers that bulked ahead and which betrayed their presence only by the sensation of space being blocked by an obstacle.

Samuel looked around for some little job to distract his

mind and dispel its morbid speculations. He dragged his chair to the window and began to clean his gun. His hands performed the accustomed task with smooth precision, their delicate movements belying the blunt insensitivity of the thick, squared fingers. It wasn't the gun, that old and valued friend, that had let him down. He polished the stock almost caressingly as though in apologetic propitiation for his own failing skills as a marksman.

The task completed to his satisfaction, Samuel sat silent, staring out of the window. The garden was blurred, indistinct, the rain-spattered window distorting its aspect. The gun was between his knees, its sheen protected from the sweat of his hand by the bunched duster, its cool, smooth barrel just touching Samuel's cheek.

In just such proximity and in this same room they had seen through a long dark night together – Samuel and his gun. But that night the gun had been loaded. The thin membrane that sealed the memory split at the touch of recollection and the wound below was as raw as the day of its infliction. It had not been lack of courage that had prevented Samuel from pulling the trigger that night but a sudden realisation that to live on into the emptiness of the next day and all the days to follow would require more bravery than swiftly to depart before the breaking of the day on which the eyes of his adored would not look. Suicide would be a vulgar epitaph to the love they had given one to the other; a cheap betrayal of the one who had not sought to die. The melodrama of the act would feed gossiping tongues with the means of conjecture so that they would clap with foul and ignorant innuendo degrading what, to Samuel, had been beautiful. From somewhere in the velvety quiet of that brooding night Samuel had found, for the sake of his dead, the courage not to make an end.

The struggle had been already over when Edwina had broken in upon his solitude, flinging wide the door as the grey light of dawn had seeped like smoke across the lawn. Seated now by the window just as he had been at the close of that long night, Samuel, in his mind's eye, saw Edwina as she had stood in front of him then in that mildewed light, his gun by that time unloaded and lying, harmless, across his knees.

The haggard lines of her face had told him that Edwina, too, had sat through the night sleepless, separate, waiting. Her voice harsh as the early cries of the starlings that had stirred to wakefulness under the eaves, she had taunted him –

'So you didn't do it! You hadn't the guts!'

Samuel had found the grace to lie. 'It was for your sake that I decided not to do it, Edwina.'

She had wept then and he had suffered her arms to clutch around him, not pulling away, his eyes closed so as not to see the bewildered pain in hers.

Samuel, his face impassive, propped the gun back in its appointed place. Slowly he mopped the sweat that beaded his forehead with the cloth which smelt familiarly of oil, and heaved himself back on his feet.

His chair pulled back to its place at his desk, Samuel fumbled for his pipe in his sagging pockets. The noise seemed unnaturally loud in the stillness of the room as he tapped out the cold dottle on the lip of the ashtray. With heavy deliberation he filled his pipe, tamping down each pinch of tobacco as though great things hung upon the undertaking. Before removing the lid from the tobacco jar he had checked that it had been firmly in place. As far as he was aware he always did ram the lid securely home – and yet there had been an occasion when he must have left it half-off – at least for long enough for that mouse to have got in.

It was the only possible explanation! The frayed sticking plaster on his thumb was a reminder of the nasty bite the little beggar had inflicted. He'd watched himself since then, confirming that he invariably replaced the lid immediately after filling his pipe. But that proved nothing because he was bringing a new consciousness to his actions. It was disturbing to suspect that he was capable of doing, or not doing things, and be left with no awareness of the action or its omission. One tolerated a degree of absent-mindedness in oneself; accepted it with irritation perhaps, but not anxiety; and then, suddenly, one found oneself examining a lapse of concentration with concern. There was a stab of fear in one's mind that one was beginning to lose one's grip; worse, that others had noticed it but refrained from remarking upon it, exchanged glances, perhaps, but no more; at least, not in one's presence.

Samuel got to his feet and prowled about the room. He glanced at the cuttings under the paperweights but felt disinclined to get down to filing any of them. In his present dispirited mood none of their topics aroused either his ire or his enthusiasm. The power of the unions, the Communist threat, the growth of Black Power, the butter mountain, teenage hooliganism, violence in the streets, the follies of the Arts Council, the abuse of Social Welfare – all had, for the moment at least, become as dust and ashes in his mouth.

He sagged against a filing cabinet and blew out a puff of smoke and was unreasonably heartened to see that a perfect smoke ring floated upwards. He essayed another but achieved nothing but a formless waver of grey cloud. That shows what happens when one tries too hard, he consoled himself. I've been working too hard – depleted my batteries. Spring can do that, too, or, so they say, pull one down; make one feel out of sorts. And there's no use denying that Wednesday didn't come up to expectations. The Board listened to what I had to say but just thanked me politely . . . too politely. Nobody likes to feel humoured, tolerated. But even if I am correct in thinking that that was their attitude, that is not at all the same thing as believing that their reaction was justified. On the contrary, it might be evidence of their crass stupidity, much more likely to be that in fact.

Seeing the change in Bunny Reeves had been a shaker too, Samuel mused. Poor old Bunny – but then his father had gone the same way, vacant, drooling by the time he was seventy. At least Bunny wasn't drooling; but it had been damned embarrassing the way he'd kept asking after Edwina, twice over the fish and again with the cheese! No good reminding him that he'd been at her funeral way back in '65. Mustn't let it prey on one's mind. Heredity, that was what explained poor Bunny's condition. All in the genes. Thank God there is nothing like that in the Gordon-Fenns. Nothing decadent there; the stuff the Empire had been built upon. Pity Edward had taken after his mother. But then, how could one have foreseen in one's youth how Edwina would turn out? His mother had seen it, of couse. She'd warned him. But what youngster worth his salt ever listened to his mother? No, these things just happened, we are all, after all, heir to the sins and follies of the flesh and must just place ourselves in the hand of the Lord.

One could be trundling along, every prospect pleasing and then – wham! Someone up there kicked over the apple-cart and one found oneself sprawling in the gutter – or as near as damn it! Not a comforting thought. On the other hand, there was solace to be derived from the knowledge that if one made a right cock-up of one's life, one could attribute one's failures to the fact that little more could be expected from a miserable sinner. But if God seemed at times frighteningly unpredictable, apparently given to visiting His subjects with bolts of wrath or compassionate forgiveness as the fancy took Him, at least His Church on earth had (until recently) provided a degree of stability in society. One had known where one stood; firmly in one's appointed and decently accepted place. A great many of the ills of society, Samuel told himself, sprang from the fact that people simply did not know their proper place in the scheme of things – and no one had the guts to spell it out.

At one time Samuel had been a fairly regular attender at the parish church and thought it a matter of justifiable pride that he had given more than he had received; and given not just in the matter of pew rent and a decent offering at Easter, but in the fact that his very presence, with the approval that that implied, must have afforded encouragement to the

Vicar. But, with the best will in the world, Samuel had found himself unable to accord that support to the new man – infected as he was by regrettable Leftish sympathies.

Still, thought Samuel, brushing away some fallen shreds of smouldering tobacco which had fallen on his waistcoat and were assailing his nostrils with the smell of singeing wool, there were advantages in dealing direct with the Head of the Firm, so to speak. From time to time Samuel did send a petition winging upwards and, if acknowledgement was tardy in arriving, that did not surprise him. Corresponding via the postal service proved a chancy enough undertaking and God only knew what hazards beset the passage of spiritual communication. Doubtless He did know – that being one of the attributes of omnipotence.

Samuel was already feeling less burdened by gloom. He was accustomed to short and mercifully infrequent attacks of despondency and was not ashamed of his moods. Secretly, he was quite proud that he was visited from time to time by an emotion which he saw himself sharing with men of superior intelligence and sensitivity. He even referred occasionally to suffering from 'the black dog' and, in case his listener failed to recognise the allusion, Samuel would kindly explain that this was how Churchill had described the affliction they endured in common.

To complete his cure, Samuel decided to check his emergency store cupboard. He was a great believer in the therapeutic benefit of activity and had once composed a long article on the subject in which, although he had stopped short of advocating the introduction of the treadmill to psychiatric hospitals, he had urged consideration of the principle implied. He still had the article in his files and enjoyed re-reading it from time to time. The editor of the national to which he had sent the article had returned it with a very courteous letter expressing his appreciation for having been given the opportunity of reading it but regretting that, owing to lack of space, he would be unable to publish it. Samuel, reading between the lines, could see quite clearly that the actual reason for the article not being published was the fact that he was not a journalist and could not, therefore, obtain membership of the union. After all, he reasoned, it was not as though the editor had rejected the article in so many words; on the contrary, he had implied that he had enjoyed reading it.

Samuel unlocked and swung open the wall-cupboard door. The orderly array on the shelves gave him a warm feeling of comfort and security. So tightly were the tins of sardines stacked that he had to remove those at the front before he could start turning each tin. This process was essential if the contents were not only to keep safely but actually to mature and improve with the passage of time. This was the treatment which had been advocated in the newspaper article which had suggested the building-up of a store of tins of sardines as a hedge against inflation. Nothing had been said about corned beef, but it seemed reasonable to suppose that what was good for the sardine was equally beneficial for meat, so after Samuel had dealt with the one category of tins, he would move on to the other. The jars of instant coffee could scarcely be thought to require regular turning – which was just as well as they were ranged in gleaming rows on the three lowest, and most inaccessible, shelves.

To the accompaniment of a hummed and individualistic rendering of 'Shenandoah', Samuel worked on, smug in the knowledge that if, or rather when, the unions chose to bring the country to its knees, the Gordon-Fenns would not starve.

Before crossing the field of her grandfather's fire, Felicity looked up and, seeing the window shut, ran on her way across the squelchy lawn where regularly spaced clumps of pampas grass hung their sodden plumes and a monkey-puzzle tree stretched dark, inhospitable arms. The wide arc of the lawn was shut off from the rest of the grounds by a tall, clipped yew hedge in the middle of which (and exactly so, the hedge having been planted with mathematical precision the year Westwood had been built) was cut an archway designed to frame a vista of order stretching beyond. In reality an unkempt wilderness now lay behind the arch, but Samuel, in a rare flight of artistic imagination, had caused a twelve-foot-wide rustic trellis to be erected and this, smothered as it was with roses, effectively hid from view the sad and sordid mess which lay beyond. The trellis was so close to the archway and the roses had flourished with such uncurbed abandon, that even the most curious and intrepid of visitors was deterred from forcing a way behind it. But Felicity side-stepped its thorny peril with a skill born of frequent practice.

'See if you can find me some parsley, dear,' her mother had said, sniffing dubiously at a piece of coley fish and deciding that a sauce pungent with herbs would be a necessity rather than an indulgence.

There had been a time when Edith had made an attempt to grow vegetables; but it had been a half-hearted one and soon abandoned. Her ineffectual scrabblings here and there on the site where once the kitchen garden had flourished had left scarcely a scar on the face of the wildwood tangle with which nature had reclaimed the ground once so assiduously cultivated. But if one knew where to look, one's search was sometimes rewarded by the discovery of a self-seeded clump of parsley, the stems grown long and fragile in their effort to lift their heads above the weeds; or a patch of grass would attract attention by the vividness of its green and would prove to be a cluster of chives fighting against the odds. Even an occasional potato haulm, pale and sickly, rubbed leaves with the foxgloves, and quite a plantation of Jerusalem artichokes flourished in amity with the bramble bushes. Felicity did know where to look and was running confidently in her wellington boots through the long grass when a baby rabbit, frozen in fear until the last moment, sprang up almost under her feet.

Felicity set off in pursuit. In the orchard she lost it, but when she reached the brick path that ran straight as a ruler through the kitchen garden she saw it ahead of her, crouched foolishly exposed. She stalked it cautiously, treading silently on the fat tussocks of moss that humped the crumbling surface of the path. Slowly, she approached near enough to see the way its little flanks heaved with the panic and exertion of its flight. Then it was off again, running straight as though mesmerised by the path and finally slipped, without pause and with space to spare, through the bars of the wrought-iron gate set in the high wall at the garden's end.

Beyond the gate lay the gardener's cottage. Felicity could not remember a time when any gardener had actually lived there, the last incumbent, Gudgeon, having died before she was born. But Gudgeon, whose time must have been fully occupied in keeping order in his employer's grounds, had so arranged his own patch of garden that it required the minimum of work. Seen like that, through the frame of the gate, it still looked attractive, even neat, in contrast to what lay behind Felicity as she stood staring intently in the hope of catching sight of a last flick of that white little scut. The sun in its sinking had at last found a chink in the cloud and a pale, watery beam touched a flowering cherry and glanced off a bright casement.

Hyacinths flowered in a stone trough by the back door of the cottage and their scent, mixed with white lilac, reached Felicity. There was another smell, too. She took a deep breath, moving her head slowly from side to side, scenting the air like a wary creature on the prowl; it was a down-to-earth domestic smell – fruitcake fresh from the oven! Lily Gudgeon, Felicity had glimpsed from time to time, plodding behind an old-fashioned whirring mower barbering her little lawn in the summer or dozing in a deck-chair with her heavy legs straight and apart. Old Lily furtively bobbing about in the jungle of raspberry canes poaching the small returned-to-the-wild berries, her head wrapped in a scarf as severely concealing as any wimple: that too Felicity had seen. One June she had come across Lily bent double, grubbing hopefully for a few spears where the asparagus still thrust delicate feathered heads through the nettles that flourished on the old beds. Lily had straightened up, hand on lower back, glared forbiddingly at Felicity and strode away with an air of authority that had defied questioning. But until this moment, and inspired by the smell of the evidence, Felicity had never thought about Lily Gudgeon having an ordinary task-filled life, an identity, there in the cottage. Lily, the subject of Grandfather's testy outbursts, Lily whose obstinacy withheld the golden key to riches, Lily the ogre saying to herself 'Today I fancy a bit of fruitcake' and setting to and baking one, all on her own in the cottage: the thought intrigued, gave to her an extra, unexpected dimension. One morning, entering Miss Frobisher's study too hastily upon her knock, Felicity had caught that lady plucking hairs from her chin with a little tweezers – Miss Frobisher had never seemed quite the same again.

Felicity pushed the iron gate; it moved slowly, heavy under her hand, its hinges keening in protest. She froze, alarmed by the noise; but nothing stirred behind the kitchen window which, as she could now see, was slightly open. Crouched, skirting round the outside of the little lawn under cover of the bushes, Felicity circled round until she stood close to the cottage wall. Confident now that she could not be seen from the windows, she straightened up, her back clammy where the disturbed shrubs had shaken droplets of water down her neck.

She edged along the wall until she could squint into the kitchen. There was a thin strain of music coming from a wireless in the room beyond, but nothing moved in the kitchen save the blue-checked curtains that flapped in the breeze from the open casement. The fruitcake, round and plump as a little footstool, stood on the draining-board, cooling.

Felicity had grasped it and had it out and hugged to her chest before she quite realised what she was doing. She could see now that it was not quite as tall as she had thought it; it stood on an old-fashioned sieve whose wooden sides were as richly brown as the cake itself. A child less well versed in the subterfuges of the prowler might have dashed wildly across the open lawn with her prize; but Felicity, her heart beating with enjoyable excitement, returned the circumspect way in which she had come, only a shivering of the lilac boughs, a trembling in the guelder roses, marking her passage.

Despite her having seemingly spent quite a time searching for it, Felicity had failed to bring any parsley in from the garden. But, thought Edith, surprised by her own flash of inspiration, the curry sauce she had made instead was quite a change. She tried another forkful – yes, it was certainly different: what one might describe as 'interesting' by any standard. Edward sometimes suggested that her cooking lacked adventure: well, she had proved that she could invent a dish – curried coley fish, a real innovation!

Samuel, Edith noted, was certainly making short work of his portion! Indeed he was, shovelling it down with a speed designed to prevent the flavour lingering on his palate and with a concentration that suggested he was acting out of a necessity born of Edith's invention.

Samuel paused for a gulp of water and a quick mopping with his napkin of his forehead, where the perspiration was beginning to trickle.

'They shove it through the letter-boxes in envelopes, y'know. Filthy swine!'

'What?' asked Edward, against his better judgement.

'I've just been reading about it.' Samuel, having disposed of the fish, had started on the rice which permitted a more leisurely approach; so it was a couple of mouthfuls later before he spoke again.

'The immigrants – when they want to get white householders out of a property.'

He took another draught of water, refilled his glass, banged the jug down on the table and, looking round at the reluctant eaters, barked –

'In envelopes. Just imagine – excrement in envelopes!'

Felicity, who had been pushing the mess about on her plate and wondering if she dared shove it over the rim and on to the carpet, pushed her plate aside.

'Really! Father!' Edward had laid down his fork as though the handle had suddenly become red hot.

Samuel grinned. 'Shakes you, doesn't it? People just don't realise what goes on. We're not told, d'you see, but by George the people in these overrun areas know all about it – up there in the Midlands.'

'Here – hold on!' he called out to Edith, seeing her hurriedly clearing the yellow-smeared plates. 'I'll have a bit more of that rice if no one else wants it – not bad, the rice. Not that there's much anyone can *do* to rice, except boil the ruddy stuff!' He had tipped the bowl over his plate and was scraping the last grains from its sides, the noise of the spoon loud in the silence.

'Fruit salad,' announced Edith, putting as much bright cheer into her voice as she could summon in the circumstances. 'Nice and refreshing after the curry, I should imagine!'

It did look quite appetising. Slices of banana, a glacé cherry or two, all a-swim with the peaches in their syrup. But there was an undercurrent to the flavour, something smoky, alien to fruit. Perhaps, thought Felicity, it's the curry that has done something rather nasty to my taste-buds, or it's the thought of that beastly thing Grandfather said and which I am doing my best not to think about. She remembered that she did have something on which she could gorge later. I can wait until the kitchen is empty, she told herself, and get hold of a knife – a nice sharp knife.

7

Felicity sat on the floor of the verandah, her feet resting on the topmost of the three wooden steps which, like the verandah itself, ran the length of the front of the tennis pavilion. Wistaria blossoms, like clusters of pale mauve grapes, shadowy in the evening light, tumbled from the roof above. To a great extent the wistaria had become the roof, its ancient gnarled stems weighing down the rustic boards, the rotted wood saved from final collapse by a network of woven tendrils. Edward, or Samuel, on their rare forays into the neglected wasteland, would pause in the tall, tangled grass where once had been the tennis court, stare glumly at the crumbling relic and declare that the old pavilion ought to be pulled down. It was unsafe, they said, a breeding place for woodworm, a spawning site for the spores of dry and wet rot and a possible refuge for rats. They never ventured inside, not trusting the distorted boards with their weight. Why, even Belinda, in the course of her short and tiresome life, had crashed through the floor of the long, narrow cabin designed to store the deck-chairs, spindly bamboo tables and tennis net. But nothing ever came of their intentions and Felicity had ceased to fear that anything would.

For as long as she could remember, the old tennis pavilion had been her private play place, her special refuge, her exclusive domain. Only Belinda had challenged Felicity's territorial rights. But after suffering the indignity of being hauled to safety with an old clothes' rope, Belinda had ceased to intrude and had thereafter bedded down in the shell of what had been the potting shed.

When Felicity had stumbled across her, one gossamer-spun summer morning, her swollen body like a plump, discarded pillow lying in the nettles under a cloud of buzzing bluebottles, she had not been grieved. Edith had mourned the waste of her capital investment but was in some measure relieved that, by an injudicious nibbling at the yew hedge, Belinda had put an end to the project which had proved doubtful from the start.

It had been Sally Pewter's mother who had started it. 'Get a goat, darling!' she had cried. 'Just think,' she had gone on, flapping her hands at the burgeoning greenery on every side, 'all this stuff kept under control *and* gallons and gallons of free milk. Cheese too and butter, once you get the knack! Such a wonderful *interest*, Edith, and I'm sure Felicity and Sally would find it great fun – animals are so *good* for children. Besides, simply everybody's into self-sufficiency these days – my word, if I had your space I'd be into hens, goats, vegetables – the lot! But, as it is, mung beans on the kitchen window-sill is about all I can manage! Of course, working all day does limit one a bit,' she had added, and Edith crossly read into the remark an inference that *she* lounged about all day reading novels and sipping the cooking sherry.

Belinda had certainly provided an interest – if one liked that sort of thing. It was interesting, for instance, to speculate on how it was that no matter how firmly her stake was driven into the ground, before long she could be discovered making inroads upon the cherished shrubs in the orderly front garden, her tethering rope trailing behind her with the stake bumping at its other end. She had been warranted as being 'in kid' but it seemed an unconscionable time in arriving and, until it did, of milk there would be no sign. The girls, after an initial tepid interest, had backed uneasily away from Belinda's cold stare and unfriendly horns. 'You'll be able to take on the milking, dear, won't that be lovely?' Edith had brightly encouraged while trying not to wonder who was going to teach her daughter the art. 'And just think how lovely the kid will be when it comes! They're so lively, baby goats – cuddly, like lambs, you know,' and, for all that

Edith knew, they might well be. 'In no time at all we'll have quite a *herd*! Sally's mother says that the health shops are crying out for goat's milk, so we'll make lots and lots of money – and all for the price of Belinda!' 'What if the kid is a "he"?' Felicity had asked in that down-putting way of the young. 'We'll cross that bridge if we meet it, dear.' 'I think salami is made out of goat,' Felicity had said with a sudden note of enthusiasm in her voice. Edith had blinked rapidly, trying to dispel a sudden vision of a little, ineptly butchered body on her kitchen table. After all, she had told herself, Felicity was only trying to be helpful and she should be grateful that she was demonstrating a practical streak in her nature – God knows, she told herself, that it's a quality sadly lacking in the present Gordon-Fenns. Dora and James must have expended so much that they had had none left over to pass on. But there were times when Felicity, for all her apparent docility, did pull one up rather smartly. 'Ruthless,' was that the word? No, that was nonsense, children were practical, that was well known and accepted, one must not, Edith rebuked herself, let one's imagination run riot. But what *did* one do with an unwanted Billy goat – did one just keep it? What about incest – or were the beasts of the field not given to that sort of decadence?

Out of gratitude for having been spared so many agonies, Edith had planted a sizeable boulder on Belinda's grave with her name painted upon it with the dregs in the tin of white gloss left over from doing the larder. The grave stood on the edge of the long grass of the tennis court which in itself was an irony, as, in life, Belinda had seldom grazed there, preferring, as she had, to chew on roses, shrubs and such of Edith's vegetables as she could locate.

Felicity was staring now straight at the place where Belinda lay. The stone was hidden from sight below the long grass, but it did not matter as her eyes were not seeking it. She was not thinking about Belinda. Felicity was not consciously thinking about anything at all. She sat very still, waiting. Butterflies, white and tortoise-shell, fluttered and spiralled round and round over a sprawling buddleia bush, settling and rising as though competing for the most favourable resting place for the approaching night. In the Sunday evening stillness, their restless movement was the only indication that time had not ceased to run. A Red Admiral, conscious perhaps of his superior splendour and offended by the vulgar milling of his drabber cousins, rose from the bush and landed on Felicity's shoulder. It could scarcely have been the colour of her blouse that had attracted him: it was off-white and outgrown, old school uniform which Edith pronounced as being quite good enough for playing about in. But over the dowdy blouse, weighing down the curled-up shrunken collar, rested four or five strings of beads glittering in the light that fell, latticed, through the overhanging wistaria. The butterfly stepped, delicately from strand to strand, probing the glossy brilliance with questing tongue as fine as a hair, but found no sweetness there. He rested on an amber sphere, wings folded, a shadow against the fine white skin of Felicity's neck.

It was not that Sally's movements were particularly clumsy, but her approach to the pavilion was beset with so many minor hazards – fallen branches that cracked underfoot, self-seeded saplings that swished as one thrust through them – that Felicity was made aware of her coming before she could see her. But it was not for Sally that she had waited in such trance-like quiet. Felicity did not know for what or for whom she had waited.

'Sorry I'm late – Mummy wanted me to help address envelopes!' Sally called out, still some yards away and doing battle with a bramble sucker which had caught in her jeans.

'Bother! I'm all caught up – honestly, it *is* awful, your garden.'

'Why don't you come the other way, then, across the tennis court, instead of down the side?'

'Because I get caught up in that trellis thing if I go that way. Besides, I never know when your grandfather might start letting off with his gun. It's terribly dangerous – Mummy says it shouldn't be allowed!'

Free now of the bramble and sucking the back of her hand where it had scratched her, Sally had arrived at the foot of the steps.

'I say, what *have* you got there?' She reached out and lifted the beads which hung to Felicity's lap.

The drowsing butterfly, disturbed, opened his wings and flew up and away. Felicity felt him brush against her neck as he rose and grabbed at him, too late. If she had caught him, she'd have put a pin through him and added him to her collection. But she was too pleased by Sally's excitement to feel disappointed at the lost opportunity.

'Look – see this, too!' She lifted the long cigarette holder from the floor.

'Golly! But what is it?' Sally was turning it round in her hands.

'A cigarette holder, silly! It's the kind they had long ago.' Felicity retrieved the holder and screwed a cigarette in place. She'd filched two from her father's case but only one had survived, unbroken, concealment in her pocket.

'But where did you get all that stuff?'

'Oh, just somewhere.' Felicity lit the cigarette with what she hoped appeared practised nonchalance, but kept her tongue humped against the roof of her mouth so that there was no danger of inhaling the smoke. Previous experiments had proved not at all pleasurable.

Sally's eyes grew round with admiration. Felicity had got to her feet and was strolling to and fro on the verandah on one of the safe planks, one foot carefully in front of the other and her pelvis thrust forward like a model on a cat walk. She twirled the beads with one hand and waved the cigarette holder with the other.

'Can I have a try?'

Generously, but only after another languid turn, Felicity ducked her head and slipped off the beads. She dropped them over Sally's head and handed her the cigarette holder.

Sally imitated Felicity's movements, but this time the beads did not hang straight down. Under her scarlet T-shirt Sally had a small, developing bosom uplifted in a 'Young Miss' bra. Felicity knew all about that bra with its lace edging and tiny rosebud right in the middle, it had been the first in their Form and the subject of much envy in the changing-room. Resting on the slight elevation, the beads swung below it in just the way Felicity intuitively knew that they should.

'You're meant to *do* something with the cigarette holder!'

'What?' asked Sally, uncertainly clenching her teeth round the holder.

'Suck it, of course! Take a really deep breath and then blow the smoke out – sort of sideways.'

Sally did; and then held on to a pillar, coughing wildly, the beads swinging madly and tears of stress trickling down her reddening cheeks.

'Never mind!' Felicity, all smug superiority, was thumping Sally's back. She plucked the cigarette holder from Sally's hand. 'You'll get the hang of it with practice,' she said, by way of comfort.

She put her arm round Sally and, the coughing at last over, they sat companionably on the steps, the beads now in a jumble on Felicity's lap and the cigarette doused because, or so she said, Felicity wanted to save it for later.

She told Sally about how beautiful Edwina had been and how she'd been the belle of every ball, men almost swooning when her eye glanced upon them as the champagne corks popped in all directions.

Sally, quite recovered and sucking a blackcurrant lozenge to soothe her affronted palate, took advantage of a pause in Felicity's eulogy to remark:

'My grandmother says that Edwina was a bit of a goer.'

'What does that mean?' Felicity was not sure that she wanted any factual information about her grandmother.

'You know . . . a flirt. Liked a lot of fun.'

'Well of course she did! Before Grandfather got poor, there was nothing to stop them having fun. I expect *your* grandmother was just jealous.'

'No, I don't think so. I think Granny was sorry for her –

83

she didn't have much fun when she was old, you know!'

'Oh that!' Felicity was cross. 'Nobody has fun when they're *old*, but if you've had lots when you were young then who cares? I'd like to have lots of money before I get old and stuffy, it's too late once you're, say, thirty.'

I won't really be sorry when Sally Pewter goes to the Comprehensive, thought Felicity, she spoils things. Perhaps I've grown out of her.

Sally, her face hidden by the curtain of her silky dark hair which fell forward as she bent to prod with a twig at an earwig, asked, with edged innocence –

'Why then, if Edwina was so wonderful, did she get married to your grandfather?'

'Well, don't you see – he was quite different then. Very handsome, you know, and always doing fun things. They used to go to places like Monte Carlo and Juan-les-Pins.' Evidence of the holidays taken in these exotic-sounding places was irrefutable, the photographs, deckle-edged, lay in drifts in the bottom drawer of the escritoire in the morning-room.

Sally was silent. She had heard her grandmother say that Samuel had been 'a well-set-up man' in his youth and Sally had sometimes wondered if her grandmother had 'fancied' Samuel when they had all been young and there really had been a tennis lawn here, in Westwood. But to try to visualise one's granny as having ever been young was a difficult jump for the imagination; Granny, Samuel and their friends, most now dead, sitting here in this very pavilion; laughing, calling out to one another, sitting round the funny little tables that mouldered now in the room at the back; cardigans slung over the backs of chairs, a gramophone – perhaps one with a horn like the ones one saw in television plays. Sally swept her hair back as though to reveal the present more clearly and jumped to her feet, squashing the earwig in the process.

'Anything to eat?' she asked, brisk and factual.

It was their custom to have little picnics, a carry-over

from the days when they had 'played house', their dolls perched drunkenly on wicker chairs and the girls themselves eating Marmite sandwiches and little dry sponge cakes in paper cups. The pavilion had not then been so decrepit. Edith had declared it to be a godsend.

'Actually, there's something rather special! No – you wait here, I'll get it!' Felicity had changed her mind about letting Sally see the whole cake. She had thought to confide the daring adventure of its acquisition but now she felt wary, no longer certain of Sally's reactions.

The pantry, at the end of the pavilion, was tiny but ample enough to have served its original purpose. It had been here that tea had been brewed, sandwiches arranged on tiered stands, lemonade glasses filled and trays loaded at those tennis afternoons, some time long ago. There was even a sink, shallow, made of stone with the look of stale veined cheese; a brass tap, standing high on its pipe above the sink, had to be turned with gentle care, as otherwise it juddered, splattering rusty water wide. There were two cupboards at eye-level with fronts of perforated zinc, still intact, proof against the wiles of mice but not of spiders. But Felicity had put the cake in a tin. Being so fresh, it proved difficult to slice but doubtless, thought Felicity, a little concerned now at the sheer daunting size of it, it would be quite mature before she had reached the end of it.

It was not possible to prepare tea. There was a primus but it was old and battered and getting hold of methylated spirit and paraffin was fraught with difficulties; Felicity knew, because she had tried. But there was a large bottle of coke, still half-full. It stood in a can of rusty water, a precaution against ants. Felicity felt relieved when the cake in its tin was safely out of sight again and loaded the tray with the bottle, mugs, the plate of cake and the little transistor radio that she kept wrapped in an old jumper on the draining-board to keep out the damp. Edith still searched, in a half-hearted manner, for the tray, and tried not to harbour uncharitable suspicions about Mrs Watson. These suspicions had been revived that very morning when Edith had discovered a bread-knife missing; it was a spare one but cherished for all that, although the staghorn handle might not be to everyone's taste.

The cake tasted very good, despite the fact that the fruit had sunk. It was that circumstance that made Sally assume that Felicity's mother had baked it. Felicity, her mouth full, felt that an ambiguous 'mmmmm' in answer was not exactly a lie – although it would not have worried her unduly to have been called upon to invent one.

Radio One filled the air with noise and Sally felt relieved that something unwelcome which had crowded close in the stillness of the garden had receded. She jumped from the top step to the ground in one and together they capered to the music on solid safe earth, the beads discarded in a little heap on the verandah floor. Felicity tripped on a mole hill and she sprawled, screaming in mock alarm, into the buddleia bush. Butterflies rose in a startled cloud and flew distractedly in all directions in the gathering dusk, the girls in shrieking pursuit.

At the other side of the yew hedge Samuel, a length of raffia clenched in his teeth and his hands gingerly teasing out a sprawl of rambler stems on the trellis, wondered for a moment whence came the faint strains of music and the eldritch cries. Cocking his head slightly, he decided that the noise seemed to be coming from the direction of the tennis pavilion. But of course – it must be Felicity and the Pewter child playing about with that damned portable wireless that Felicity kept in the pavilion! Extraordinary what passed for music nowadays, thought Samuel as the thin throb of the music splintered the quiet of the evening. Nobody wrote decent tunes any more – songs with words which stuck in your mind, melodies that one could hum, catchy little numbers with rhythm. Carefully he tied the rose to the trellis and lowered his arms which were aching with the unaccustomed exercise. He should have pruned the ramblers in the autumn, it was too late now with the little fat buds almost ready to burst into full flower. Ivor Novello, that was the name of the chap whose songs used to be all the rage, that had been stuff worth listening to! And what was that thing which Edwina had been keen on singing . . . 'Oh I love to climb a mountain and to reach the highest peak, but it doesn't thrill me half as much as dancing cheek to cheek!' She'd had a jolly sort of voice, light but with a haunting lilt.

He stepped back to look at the effect his work had had on the thicket of rose branches. Not much to show for it, he admitted to himself, no knowing where Paul's Scarlet left off and Dorothy Perkins began. He'd need to put in some more work on it in the morning when the light would be better. The trouble was that his heart wasn't in gardening any more; it made him feel lonely, bereft. Plants were heartless things – they went on growing, regardless. Hearing another generation playing music and larking about in the pavilion was strangely disturbing. But it was good to know that Felicity was having a bit of fun; it must be lonely for her being an only child. Edith ought to stir herself a bit, take more interest in Felicity; give her a party now and again to encourage other children to come around – it wasn't as though Westwood didn't offer space and to spare! Samuel tied in another branch, peering intently in the failing light. Edwina had been right about Edith, she'd got her measure from the beginning.

Samuel could see Edwina now as she had looked when she had pronounced judgement on her future daughter-in-law. Briefly restored after a spell at the Health Farm in preparation for Edward's wedding, she had sat opposite him in the drawing-room, flipping through a magazine in that restless way she had had, riffling the pages like a sharper with a deck of cards; edgy, tense but with that quality of clear perception that hung around her for the first few days after the completion of one of her 'cures'. It wasn't a state that persisted; later the melancholy mien would engulf her and then would follow the furtive return to the bottle and the hectic manic spiral which would lift her frighteningly out of control before the inevitable downward plunge which would set in motion, yet again, the whole dreary and desperate cycle. But that evening Edwina's senses had been sharp, her vision clear. She had spent the afternoon helping Edward and Edith with their guest list and the youngsters had driven away in a haze of bright and optimistic goodwill.

'I asked Edward, when I got him alone in the kitchen, what it was that attracted him to Edith. Do you know what he said?' Edwina had asked, the glossy pages of the magazine flopping slap, slap, under her unquiet hands. 'He said that it's her air of calm, her quality of tranquillity that draws him. I suppose that would appeal to him – coming from a household like this! Just what he would look for in a wife, calm and tranquillity; qualities that imply capability and strength.'

'Well, that's all right, then!' Samuel had answered, weary after an afternoon of bright chatter and eager for a little peace and quiet. 'Sounds as though she'll suit him very well.'

'But he's quite mistaken, of course,' Edwina continued, as though he had not spoken. 'She's not at all what he thinks. Edward's in love and naturally sees in her what he wants to see – what he needs to see. That girl isn't capable . . . not really tranquil either. Edith is self-absorbed. You'll see, Samuel, I know I'm right. Self-absorbed . . . and devoid of spunk. Ah well – ' and Edwina had flung the magazine carelessly from her so that it landed on the floor and sent her sealyham into a frenzy of yapping, 'everyone must be free to pick his own path to disaster. "Hell" is written on the back of all the signposts anyway!'

Samuel withdrew his hand from the roses with too sharp a movement and a thorn tore across a finger. A sated bumble-bee, bedded down for the night in the honeysuckle that entwined the rambler, tumbled from the blossom so roughly shaken by his blundering hand. It fell to the ground and lay on its back in the grass. Samuel plucked a leaf and, legs astride to keep his balance, bent laboriously and held the leaf above the bee's wildly questing legs until they made a hold and he was borne safely upward and gently restored, ruffled but unharmed, to his fragrant shelter.

'There you are, old fellow, all tucked up for the night and none the worse!' Samuel murmured. The honeysuckle trembled and spilt its scent upon the air. Samuel briefly closed his eyes as though waiting for pain to spend itself – as though it ever would, the pain of memory that haunted this garden.

Samuel's secateurs lay at his feet where he had dropped them when he had bent down, but he decided to let them lie until the morning. He certainly wasn't going to risk bending down again like that – the darkling sky over Westwood was suddenly alive with black dots. Liverish spots, perhaps? There had been a great deal of fat on that lamb casserole which Edith had dished up at dinner (surely she could have trimmed the meat before cooking it?). It was a comfort when it dawned upon him that the dancing black specks were not, after all, an optical delusion but were bats flying out from the attic just as they had done in the gloaming of spring and summer evenings for as long as Samuel could remember. But I used to be able to hear their squeaks, he thought, as he watched them flit silently overhead. Felicity's ears must still be young enough for her to hear them. I must ask her sometime, he thought, lumbering across the lawn towards the light that streamed from the uncurtained morning-room window. But he knew that it was unlikely that he would ask her. Communication with those not of his own generation had never come easily to Samuel. Too late to try to do anything about that, or any other of one's failings, reflected Samuel, glad to find some consoling factor in growing old. Too late to change one's spots! But how much easier things were for the leopard who, never having questioned his condition, had been spared the vain effort of trying to change it.

8

Edward was doodling on the pad by his telephone: first a little square that sprouted a leg in the last corner which started another, slightly larger box. Across, down, sideways and up, short, jerky strokes, the pen never leaving the paper. Lily Gudgeon, he brooded, was not just a stubborn, absurd, old woman. She was malicious and crafty. Her veiled threat had not been committed to paper, but had been hissed in his ear over the telephone. His letter to her had in no wise been offensive. If she did not wish even to look at the bungalow that he and Samuel were prepared to buy in order to provide her with an alternative home, then no more need be said. But she had chosen to say more.

The death of a client and the fact that the heir lived in New Zealand and desired only a quick sale of his legacy, had seemed so fortunate. The bungalow which comprised the legacy was tiny, well-kept, easy to run, near the shops and with a bus-stop within yards. No stairs to tax elderly legs and the curtains and carpets included in the sale. But Lily had turned the proposition down flat. 'Take my advice' (not the most fortunate of phrases to address to a professional giver of advice), she had added, 'and don't try dragging *me* into court! There are things I could tell about your precious family that you wouldn't like aired in public. Very nasty things – you just ask your father, young man!' and then she had hung up on him! Poisonous bitch, he thought.

It would be gossip about his mother. It could only be that. There was nothing else – surely?

The Gudgeons, Edward reflected, had been brought to Westwood by Samuel at the end of the war, in 1945. Mother was by then certainly over-fond of a drink. 'A bit of a tippler' one might say – but not to an extent that would really attract notice. Some years were to pass before it became apparent that Edwina had what friends referred to as 'a problem'. By the late Fifties, friends were few and, such as remained, had transferred their charity to Samuel.

There had been remissions, not spontaneous, but resulting from ever more frequent withdrawals to the type of establishment that catered for the needs of such as Edwina. 'Edwina's taken herself off to that bloody Health Farm again. The vanity of women, eh? Never gives in, y'know, won't accept the wrinkles and the sags of middle age. Costs me a pretty penny, Edwina's looks, I can tell you!' Samuel would bluff it out and his listeners would stare, embarrassed, into their dry sherries and wonder, uneasily, if they should stick to Bitter Lemon.

Edward had come home once, unannounced, for the weekend, unaware that his mother was 'having a bit of a bout'.

In the middle of the night he had been awakened by her screams. She had been standing, naked, halfway down the stairs, a jumble of shoes clutched to her breasts with one hand while with the other she was flinging them, one after another, at the alabaster bowl of the hall's light fitment. Her aim was so erratic that he would not have guessed what was her target had it not been indicated by the direction of her wide-eyed stare. She had wriggled from his arm, as thin and lithe as an elver and, stumbling over scattered shoes, he had pursued her through the moonlit rooms, her sealyham yapping excitedly at his heels. Racing back across the hall she had cut her feet on a jagged piece of a shattered crystal flower vase which had been knocked to the floor by one of the flying shoes. Weeping, she had collapsed to the floor to lie sprawled among the broken flowers. Edward had carried her, a light burden, up the stairs. His father had sat, silent, on the top step. Samuel had been wearing his dressing-gown and had had slippers on his feet; he had taken his time to arrive at the scene. It was clear that the familiarity of such occurrences had robbed Samuel's reactions of any sense of urgency.

Edward had sat with his mother until she had at last fallen asleep. She had confided to him about the snakes that hid by day in the lamp bowl and, under cover of darkness, slithered out, undulated under her door and glided into her bed where they obscenely invaded her body while she slept.

Doubtless, Edward acknowledged in his thoughts, Lily Gudgeon could, if she chose, revive old horrors, tear open old wounds; make public that which one had hoped was decently buried. But would it matter? Yes, Lily knew it would prove painful for Samuel and, to say the least, embarrassing for Edith and a terrible revelation for Felicity. People would be sympathetic – but that could well prove to be the worst part to bear.

Edward's train of thought was broken by Miss Giles coming in with his coffee and a plain tea biscuit. It was a trifling matter, too petty to broach, but surely it was beyond the rules of chance that, in all the years since he had joined the firm, all Edward ever received from the Tin of Assorted was a cream cracker or a plain tea. The chocolate-coated biscuits found their way to the Senior Partner's plate and the Chief Clerk had his partiality for the jammy-centred gratified. What, Edward used to wonder before he became reconciled to her resentment, what had he ever done to offend Miss Giles?

Miss Giles was still standing there, looking sourly at this married, middle-aged mouse who had crept into the office following the death of poor old Mr Fordyce, filling the vacancy which had belonged, of right, to the attractive young man of her dreams who would have swept her away from her typewriter and the dusty old deed-boxes for ever. Miss Giles had left such dreams behind her, but the conviction that Edward was a usurper remained.

'You've not forgotten, have you, that you've got Mr Waller coming at 11.30? I expect it's too late for you to start your dictation before then, so I'll come back after he's left.' Her eyes rested briefly on his untouched In Tray and then slid to the defaced message pad. 'And you asked me to remind you that you won't be going home for lunch today.'

He wouldn't? Then he remembered. 'Thank you, Miss Giles, don't know how we'd get along without you, eh?' He was smiling at her in an almost ingratiating way and receiving back her stony stare – which he knew was no more than he deserved.

Yes, of course. Edith had warned him days ago that he would get no luncheon at home on Thursday, had reminded him of the fact at breakfast. Edith was having an affair today. Affair? That was what came of thinking about his mother. God knows she'd had affairs in plenty. In the war. Westwood filled with billeted young officers, his mother the envy of her friends who'd been landed with snotty-nosed evacuees. Coming home for the school holidays and aching with love for this mother who suddenly looked so much younger, so beautiful and so full of fun. Jealous, too, of the men who seemed to know her so much better than he did. But excited, too, to be on the edge of such unaccustomed gaiety. The house, freed at last by her death of his grand-mother's forbidding presence, had quite a different atmos-phere. There were tennis parties again, lots of them all through the summer holidays; but they were much jollier than had been the occasional ones given and overlooked by Grandmother. There had been no shortage of strong arms to push the roller and mark the court. Father, himself away on Army service, had been absent. There had been dancing in the drawing-room, the carpet rolled up and the radiogram belting out. It had been Edwina's war work – keeping the dear boys happy, as she had put it. All the Winnies organised into helping to do their bit – but only up to a point, the best bits being reserved for Edwina herself.

Lily Gudgeon might rake over these dead scandals too, thought Edward, sourly. The gossip had still been fresh when Lily and her husband had arrived at Westwood. For some time after the war had ended, old friends of Edwina's had turned up for the occasional weekend, 'nostalgia trips' his mother had called them. Well, none of it would be news to Samuel but, naturally, he would prefer not to be reminded.

Edith's 'affair' at Westwood this morning was an eminently respectable one. A coffee-morning cum bring-and-buy to boost the funds of the Winifred Coldthorpe Society – affectionately known to its members as the 'Winnies' and referred to by those outside its membership as the wcs; their use of such a vulgar abbreviation being evidence of their unfitness to be extended an invitation to join. One of the great attractions of the Society was that membership was not to be had for the asking, but was graciously conferred.

Winifred Coldthorpe had been a lady of philanthropic persuasion and the Society which bore her name had been founded at the turn of the century to administer the estate which she had left to charity and to continue her good work. Winifred herself had been concerned with providing boots and woollen vests to the children of the poor of the town, coal and parcels of tea to their elders and Christmas puddings to the inmates of the Poor House. Her successors sought chinks in the Welfare Services and did their laudable best to fill them. Edward's grandmother had been an early president, so it was only fitting that Edith should fill a place on the committee. Edith herself would have preferred to have devoted the time expected of one in her position to be given to the cause of charity, to work in the field of animal welfare. Samuel, however, had pointed out to her that, as the committees in that sphere were composed almost entirely of members of the hunting and blood sports fraternity, her worth would be unlikely to receive recognition. Edith did not seek recognition, but Samuel's advice had scared her off from that particular field of endeavour. She appreciated that, if Samuel's assessment was correct, then it was scarcely her métier. Her own accomplishment in the equine world had advanced no further than, as a four-year-old, stuffing her Shetland pony with sugar lumps in an endeavour to make him so fat that even her parents would be forced to realise that to perch her on its broad back would be an act of dangerous folly.

Edward sighed and reached for the Waller file, neatly marked up by the maddeningly efficient Miss Giles. Mr Waller was charged with indecent exposure. Legal Aid, of course. Edward seemed to be entrusted only with the Legal Aid cases – still, it made a welcome change from the eternal and boring business of property conveyancing.

He would, he decided, treat himself to a really good lunch – dinner would be bound to be a scrap affair with Edith intent on using up the left-overs from the morning's function.

9

Edith stood half in and half out of the drawing-room, causing a degree of awkwardness in the exits and entrances of her guests, but believing it was her duty as hostess to be accessible.

By taking a couple of steps backwards she could just see Samuel seated at a little table inside the open front door. He was taking the entrance money and was bursting with genial *bonhomie* of a grandfatherly, doggish order. He looked very spruce, hair plastered in dampish strands over his bald patch and cheeks so glowing and shiny that they might have been vigorously buffed for the occasion. Like a small boy at a party, well brushed and outwardly biddable, Samuel's manner gave no hint of the tantrums that had gone before.

He really had been very tiresome, thought Edith, irritated by the almost skittish air with which Iris Thomson was reacting to Samuel's heavy banter. But then, everyone acknowledged that Iris was a rackety, feckless sort of woman. Jeans at her age! It was a pity that she couldn't see her rear view. But Samuel was regarding it with a sardonic air as she wobbled towards the dining-room with her contribution for the stall. Probably runny marmalade again, thought Edith, smug in the knowledge that her own preserves could not be faulted in that respect; bouncy perhaps, but runny, never.

Samuel had failed to put in an appearance at breakfast and, when Felicity had been sent to see what was wrong, he had given her a message to the effect that he felt a bit 'done-in' and wanted his breakfast sent up on a tray. Later, he had recovered sufficiently to lock himself in the bathroom for quite an hour, singing at the top of his voice and deaf to

Edith's frantic knocking at the door as the time for the arrival of the Winnies grew ever nearer. The bathroom, so diligently spruced up for the occasion, had been left in a ghastly shambles. Bath-scummy and unrinsed, with horrid grey hairs sprouting from the plug hole and Edith's choicest soap (the French Gardenia) stuck like some gelatinous growth to the bottom of the bath; the floor awash and the towels (Edith's best, naturally) flung about in sodden twists. Toenail clippings had been scattered in horny crescents over the wet floor in such profusion that one was inclined to wonder if Samuel possessed more than the normal complement of toes; at least their presence dispelled the uncharitable suspicion that his legs ended in cloven hooves. He had trimmed his moustache over the washbasin and had left the prunings speckled over its surface. To crown it all, when Edith, flustered and fussed from cleaning up his mess, had eventually arrived downstairs Samuel, immaculately groomed, had chided her with 'Cutting it a bit fine, aren't you?'

'Edith dear, where shall I put this?'

A cake, glassy in its polythene shroud, was held out in front of her.

'Ruth! How lovely that you could come, dear! The cake stall is in the dining-room this year – less draughty than the hall.'

Oh dear, thought Edith, realising too late that Ruth would probably feel hurt because she had failed to say something complimentary about her contribution. It must certainly have taken a great deal of Ruth's time; that elaborate maze of walnuts and angelica on the top and all those butter cream rosettes crowned with dreadful little silver balls.

The drawing-room really doesn't look too bad when it is full of people, reflected Edith, making a determined effort to keep her mind on the matter in hand. It really looks rather . . . nice. In fact, now that all the tedious preparations are behind me, I'm really quite enjoying it all! So many nice women who have bothered to come and have paid one another the compliment of taking care over their appearance.

Lots of pretty clothes, everyone smiling at one another. A faint scent in the air – nothing obtrusive or vulgar, just a smell of good-quality face-powder and discreetly perfumed soap mingled with the scents wafting through the open french window from the garden. Freshly mowed grass, that was it; the milkman had made a really good job of the lawn! Some of the women had already gone outside and were strolling about – such a pretty picture they made! Yes, it was all very civilised. Edith felt a warm swelling of affection for her own sex and gave Miss Swan, who seemed to be raising her coffee cup in a sort of jolly waving gesture, the benefit of her sudden sweet smile. Miss Swan, who had been trying to squint at the maker's mark on the bottom of her cup, smiled uncertainly back and then transferred her confused gaze to Dora's portrait, which only made her feel more guilty.

Dear Miss Swan, thought Edith, she always supports our little 'do's'. Every year, without fail. Of course, by its very nature and the fact that it is a morning function, it is not surprising that most of the guests are middle-aged . . . and some a good deal more than that. Quite a number are retired spinsters – like Miss Swan who used to be a history mistress at High Beeches – nowadays I suppose one should refer to them as 'bachelor career women' rather than spinsters. Widows too, glad of every chance to socialise, delighted to fill their engagement books. But no! That is an odiously patronising fashion in which to regard them. Just the smug sort of attitude Samuel subscribes to – as though women bereft of male support are in some way diminished! In fact, thought Edith, her gaze roving over the elderly spinsters and widows, the opposite seems to be the case. They all look very competent, contented and very much in possession of themselves. More sure of themselves than are their married contemporaries, really. Perhaps only in self-sufficient independence do women reach their full potential. But surely that was nonsense? Certainly I wouldn't wish to be without Edward, thought Edith, her hand flying to her neck as she hastily dismissed the better-unexamined train of thought.

There was quite a sprinkling of young married women, Edith noted with approval. That was always an encouraging sight – one would hate the Winnies to become a Society composed mainly of the . . . well, more mature. People said that the young took social obligation, the need for charitable activities, less seriously than their elders; well, all the more reason that one should teach by example!

Young Mrs Woodward had come; now, if anyone needed to be taken out of herself it was young Mrs Woodward. She was leaning against the piano, dropping cigarette ash on the carpet and looking very fraught. She generally looked like that, but today she also looked rather ill. Well, that was scarcely to be wondered at; the way she conducted her life couldn't do anyone any good. Sleeping pills, pep pills to get her through the day, gin and tonics in the evening to sustain the sparkle. None of it was a secret – she agonised interminably about what she termed her 'hang-ups' to anyone who would lend a sympathetic ear. She had Clare cornered now, poor Clare. Never mind, Mrs Woodward would have to leave shortly – her little boys would have to be collected from nursery school by midday. The strange thing was that she blamed her neurotic state on her being over-educated for the role of wife and mother! Which did she regret, her Double First or her marriage? If she ever poured her grievances into Samuel's ear, his triumph at such confirmation of his theories would be too horrible to contemplate.

My God, thought Edith, shifting her gaze from Mrs Woodward's agitated mouth, I do believe that ghastly woman has just gone into the dining-room! Every year Lily Gudgeon managed to get wind of the correct date and regularly turned up. How she had the face! Edith's own got quite flushed at the effrontery of the uninvited guest. But as long as the invitation cards bore the words 'do feel welcome to bring your friends' there was really nothing one could do about it. Miss Sinclair was always sent an invitation. One could not very well *not* send Miss Sinclair an invitation as she donated most generously to the Winnies' raffles; her gifts were usually in the form of unsold Christmas stock from her little sweet shop, but very welcome for all that. Besides, the demands of the shop on Miss Sinclair's time were such that one was confident that she would never actually take advantage of the invitation. The invitation list was so discriminatingly composed that Miss Sinclair could scarcely be blamed for boasting a little about her invitation and that was obviously how Lily Gudgeon was informed about it. But one could scarcely ask Miss Sinclair not to mention the matter to Lily Gudgeon – that would be so pointed, so undignified.

Edith crossed the hall to the dining-room, avoiding looking towards Samuel in case he bellowed something rude to her about the arrival of Lily.

There she was, large as life, holding forth about something to the little bunch of women round the cake stall. Lily had a basket with her but if her previous form was anything to go by, she wouldn't buy anything at this stage in the proceedings. Lily delayed her purchasing until later in the expectation of snapping up the unsold jars of jam and the less appetising-looking cakes at reduced prices. Edith pursed her lips with vexation. The trouble was that Monica (who already looked as though she was longing to kick off her shoes) just didn't have the stamina to stick it out; she flagged too early and started selling off cheap so that she could clear her stall. But one had to make allowances – varicose veins were a dreadful affliction. Monica had been in charge of the cake stall at the Winnies' functions for as long as any of the committee could remember and no one had the heart to tackle her about giving up that particular responsibility. Hints, of course, were dropped – a chair was placed at the back of her stall; but Monica ignored both hints and chair.

The White Elephant stall was doing well. It generally did, but it was a stall which could produce difficulties. Edith's quick appraisal of the articles on offer was wary. On one occasion she had been disconcerted to see a familiar object among the discarded household goods. It had been a bulb bowl of a rather poisonous green which she herself had given to Joyce as a Christmas present. It had been embarrassing to see Miranda's eye also light up with recognition. Only at that moment of mutual recognition had Edith recalled that it had been Miranda who had originally given it to her. This year there were several items which Edith was sure she had seen only weeks before at an NSPCC Bring and Buy; and, yes, there was that bottle of Verbena Bath Salts which had been going the rounds for years – its blue satin bow was a trifle limp and shop-soiled with the passage of time but its contents were as biliously bright as ever. It was as though the rules of some esoteric sub-culture were being observed, where token gifts, never designed for actual use or enjoyment, were solemnly bought and exchanged in the knowledge that, before long, they would find their way back into the stream of circulation; but it was all in a good cause.

A great many used and empty cups littered the sideboard : whatever was Mrs Watson doing? Edith wondered. For that matter, several of the helpers were conspicuous by their absence. The food trolley was in need of re-stocking – it was not possible that all those egg-and-cress sandwiches and home-made little cakes stacked high on the kitchen table had been used up already! What Edith feared must have happened : the helpers must be standing around chatting in her kitchen, a kitchen whose shabby inadequacies Edith did not wish exposed to the eyes of the curious. Next time, Edith decided, I shall put a table across the doorway and Mrs Watson can hand things over to the helpers who will then have no excuse or opportunity to enter where their presence is not desired.

Edith hurried on her way to the kitchen to put an end to any leisurely appraisal that might be going on. Samuel's bellow reached her just before she whisked out of sight. She turned back, knowing that he was quite capable of continuing to bawl her name in that imperious fashion until she came to heel like a docile gun dog.

'Want to stretch my legs for a bit!' Samuel was lumbering to his feet, reaching in his pocket for his pipe. 'You'd best take over here – although I don't expect there are many still to come.'

'I can't possibly!' Just thinking about working out the correct change put Edith in quite a flutter. Twenty-two and a half pence was such an awkward entrance charge – but the treasurer had been adamant. The figure had been carefully calculated to allow for a percentage inflation rise on the simpler round sum of the past. Besides, Edith felt uncomfortable about extorting money from friends at her own front door – even if it was for the Winnies and did include the cost of as much coffee as the guests cared to drink. But it ruined the whole illusion of gracious hospitality.

'I have to see to things in the kitchen!' she pleaded, remembering that this was indeed the case.

'Very well. I'll get Mrs Casement to stand in. Just stay here a sec, and keep an eye on the cash until she comes!'

'Really, Samuel! As though any of the guests would – '

'Don't take anything for granted these days, my girl! The world's become nothing more than a bally jungle – a corrupt, stinking jungle!' Samuel strode off, his head enveloped in a blue cloud of tobacco smoke as though he were indeed intent upon keeping malarial mosquitoes at bay.

Mrs Casement reported eagerly for duty, taking with her a fat book of raffle tickets.

'Catch them while they've got their purses out!' she boomed, showing a large number of strong yellow teeth.

Just as I thought! Edith told herself, finding Miranda, Joyce and Beth all chatting in her kitchen. The chat faded and was replaced by bright vague smiles when she appeared, always an alarming sign.

'I was just saying, Edith, how lucky you are to have a really *old-fashioned* kitchen!' Joyce was running a beautifully manicured finger along the dingy cream paintwork of a wall cupboard.

'It's all the thing now, y'know. I'm trying to talk Jack into replacing my units with natural pine. There's a little man in Brighton who does them very reasonably in wood that's specially treated to look old and worn – "distressed", I think one calls it. It would be so easy to strip yours off, darling!' That was true – the paint having almost worn away; the knots showed through like the freckles on an old skin.

'You've got lipstick on your teeth,' Miranda was glaring at Joyce, who seemed not to notice. She had stepped back from the cupboard and was gazing around the big, ugly kitchen in the manner of an interior designer facing up to a challenge.

'Such space!' Joyce crowed. 'But then you've got your wonderful Mrs Watson to keep it in order!'

Mrs Watson was loading a plate with sandwiches, her hand did not pause, but her lips tightened in an ominous way.

'So wise not to have gadgets or mechanical things – domestic help is so much better. When we had old Mary it was such bliss! Do you know, she even used to darn Jack's handkerchiefs. Beautiful darns – can you imagine?'

Joyce was fond of sentences which began 'when we' and also inclined to sing the praises of 'old Mary' more often than was good for the patience of her listeners.

'If you really want to help, you can take these through for the trolley.' Beth thrust a plate of sandwiches at Joyce with a nice precision that ensured that the blob of butter which she had spotted was resting on the rim, was rubbed against Joyce's dress of *eau de nil* linen.

The committee had never forgiven Joyce over the business of the Worcester bowl although the incident had occurred three years previously. The bowl had been given to the White Elephant stall by Kate Pewter and Joyce had bought it for seventy-eight pence. Almost immediately, she had sold it for twenty-eight pounds to the peculiar young man with one ear-ring who owned the antique shop in the High Street. Joyce had openly boasted of this feat as evidence of her superior knowledge of antique china. When it became clear that neither the funds of the Winnies nor Kate Pewter were to benefit from the windfall, a special meeting of the full committee had been convened; well not quite the full committee, Joyce herself having naturally been excluded. It had been decided that Joyce should be invited to resign, her behaviour having sullied the reputation which the Winnies so jealously cherished. But, in the end, no one was prepared actually to bell the cat. Joyce remained and, as a focal point for mutual dislike, played an important role as a factor of unification among the Winnies.

The committee would remain for luncheon after everything was over and the debris of the morning cleared up. Edith, unable to clear the kitchen of lingering helpers, was glad of her foresight in having filled the sherry decanter while she had had the kitchen to herself. It would have been embarrassing to have been caught out decanting the Cyprus Medium Dry (special offer of the week). Particularly so as, when having been complimented upon the same brand on a previous occasion, she had hinted vaguely about the reliability and acumen of Edward's London merchant.

Samuel, who had managed to nip upstairs for something a little more stimulating, was now sipping his coffee with every appearance of benign appreciation. He had stood himself by the open french window, an excellent vantage point from which to observe all the guests. He had discarded his pipe in favour of a cigar, a generous gesture on his part, as he believed that ladies, or at least those who could with correctness be so described, enjoyed the aroma of a good Havana. The breeze was wafting the smoke into the drawing-room and as more and more of the women decided to take their coffee out on to the lawn, Samuel was able to exchange pleasantries with them *en route* to the fresh air, and believed it was the prospect of that brief encounter that had led their steps in his direction.

If one had not known to the contrary, Kate Pewter mused, one might well assume that Samuel was a retired general. He really wears very well, she thought, so upright, the grey moustache so neatly trimmed and the blue eyes so lively.

The colour was too high, but of a quality that suggested it could have been acquired on the grouse moors. The belly too large but that, of itself, in no way undermined his general air of authority. Frightful old *poseur*! But Kate's little smile was one of exasperated fondness – the fondness one entertains for things, or people, who have been around in one's life for a long time. She felt much the same brief surge of exasperated affection towards the terrible old woman with the squint and the Trilby hat who kept the second-hand bookstall in the market, and for the arthritic, decaying sheepdog who sprawled on the floor of the fishmonger's shop. The landscape would be less familiar without them and as one grew older the familiar became more precious.

Kate wondered how many of the women remembered, or had ever known, that Samuel's military experience had been limited to the war years when he had served (somewhere in Norfolk, if her memory did not fail her) in the clothing section of the Ordnance Corps. He had been a captain, non-substantive, by the time victory had been achieved. Perhaps the Military had thought that keeping records of boots and vests was an appropriate fate for a failed commodity broker past his prime!

'Kate! How splendid to see you!' Samuel had flung his arms wide, scattering ash over Miss Swan's blue rinse and causing his cup to slide alarmingly in its saucer. Kate relieved him of the china and, ducking her head a little as she placed it down on a side-table, received on her forehead the kiss that had been aimed at her cheek.

'Where have you been hiding yourself, eh?'

'Oh I've been buying this and that at the cake-stall – don't bother baking much these days, not worth it on one's own.'

'Nice to see people about the place again – quite like old times, what?'

No, not like old times at all, thank God, thought Kate, remembering being closeted in this drawing-room with her mother and other ladies of Dora's select circle on that lady's

At Home afternoons. Tiered cake-stands, china tea in the Crown Derby and the sun shining outside the closed windows; Dora had believed that exposing oneself to the sun was a vulgar and unhealthy practice. Later had come the parties 'thrown' by Edwina and Samuel – but in their own, and very different way, these had seemed no less terrible to Kate.

She smiled up at Samuel. 'The old days are gone, Samuel, and I for one don't harken after them – I'm reasonably content with my present!'

Samuel scowled. 'Oh, so you say, so you say! But I can't believe you enjoy living in that poky little bungalow; how you could have allowed them to tear down the Chase and cover the ground with a sprawl of bloody rabbit-hutches, I'll never understand.'

'Well, for a start, my dear little bungalow is far from poky. I've never been more comfortable in my life and it wasn't a case of my "allowing" anyone to pull down the Chase – I instigated it, as you very well know; and the people who live in what you choose to call "the rabbit hutches" make jolly good neighbours! Besides, you old hypocrite,' she added, wagging a plump, pink finger under his nose, 'you know damned well that you can scarcely wait to sell your own acres to the developers!'

'Wouldn't pull Westwood down, though! I was never one to give in and run – *you* should know that, Kate.'

Kate knew nothing of the kind, suspecting that Samuel's prowess at holding on depended on someone else manning the ramparts.

'It's only a fool who tries to withstand a rising tide, Samuel.'

Samuel, as though Kate had not spoken, went on –

'Fat chance I have of getting the developers in as long as that bloody woman stays put in the cottage. It's a question of access, d'you see? I'll be dead and buried before she chooses to shift her fat . . . to see reason,' he ended, lamely, seeing a certain glint in Kate's eye.

Edward and Edith were far too soft with him, Kate thought.

He's the kind who needs standing up to. The more people let him get away with his boorishness, the more he despises himself. Dora, in her way, had been right. I could have managed Samuel – up to the point where no woman could change Samuel. Thank God I never felt any temptation to try!

'How's Felicity these days?'

'Oh she gets along all right, I suppose. Not here today, of course – school, I expect.'

'She's going to be a lovely woman, Samuel. She's inherited a lot of Edwina's looks.'

'Ah.'

'She's going to miss Sally. Never the same when children move to different schools. You'd heard that Sally's moving to the Comprehensive?'

Samuel nodded. 'Children! Don't know why we have 'em. Like cats, let them loose and you never know what they'll come home with.'

Kate took this as an oblique reference to her daughter-in-law whose decision it had been to move Sally to the Comprehensive, but she refused to be drawn on the subject of either her son or his wife.

'Ever thought of sending Felicity to boarding-school? It could be lonely for her here – an only child.' She was holding Samuel's eyes with her own, hoping in some way to convey the thoughts which she could scarcely clarify and would certainly stop short of putting into words – even had she been able to. Get the child out of this place.

The drawing-room almost empty now; Kate could feel the indefinable chill of Westwood creeping at her back. It's only the warmth of the sun drawing the damp from the walls, she told herself uneasily, moving into the golden oblong of warm light in front of the window.

'Out of the question, old girl. It's a matter of money. Besides, it's not as if it was a boy! Anyway, none of my damned business.'

Nor mine, thought Kate, accepting the heavy-handed hint.

As though to soften the rebuke, Samuel had slipped his arm round where her waist used to be. His finger gave her a little squeeze – at least she thought they did, but it was difficult to tell through her corset. I should never have looked him straight in the eye like that, she chided herself.

'Tell you what, Katy! Once we're in the money again, I'll put something aside to see Felicity all right – invest it for her myself. Edward's got no flair for money, too timid. And' – Yes! He *was* squeezing her, kneading with his fingers with all the finesse of a farmer sizing up fatstock – 'I'll tell you what! I'll stand you a holiday – Porto Fino, what? Remember that time the four of us went? D'you know, I've almost forgotten the taste of real coffee – Edith uses that powdered muck, bloody gnats' piss! And the lobsters – my God, the lobsters!'

Samuel's eyes had assumed the misty, unfocused stare of a visionary and the arm around Kate slackened its hold. The hairs in his nostrils trembled as he took a deep breath preparatory to heaving a dramtic sigh. Kate moved a couple of paces away from him: the lawn with its sprinkling of guests was a pleasanter sight on which to rest her gaze. Porto Fino. Breakfast on the terrace of the Splendide, blue hydrangeas spilling with almost vulgar exuberance down the slope. Edwina's laughter slicing through the peace and sending the little green lizards scuttling. Kate remembered, too, how, with the heartless self-centredness of the young, she and Peter had found their joy in one another enhanced by sharing their holiday with Samuel and Edwina. She felt slightly guilty, even now, as she remembered their shared glances: Peter's barely lifted eyebrow directing her attention to Samuel's gaze which, when not on his food, wandered speculatively and fastened with desire on bodies lissom and graceful enough in their own way but not, to the casual observer, competing with the attractions of Edwina. She smiled a little now, catching the ghost of Peter's quizzical look from the corner of her eye.

Samuel, back in the present, and misinterpreting Kate's

smile (not unnaturally, as no one else was in their immediate vicinity), said with eagerness, 'What d'you say, eh? Worth thinking about anyway, what?'

'Don't go counting your chickens, Samuel. I usually go to the Greek islands nowadays. Less spoilt, you know.'

Yes, thought Samuel, annoyed at having exposed himself to rebuff, so she does – not to mention Switzerland in the winter. Overheads on that damned bungalow of hers must be a flea-bite compared to keeping up Westwood; good lump in the bank too, if the rumoured sum she had got for selling up was anywhere near correct. Well, it had only been an idea. Probably enjoy himself more on his own, anyway. But there were decided advantages in being accompanied when venturing outside England. There were unpredictabilities abroad. He certainly wouldn't take Edward and Edith along! One of the many advantages that improved finances would bring would be the opportunity to get them out of his hair. Edward would just have to learn to stand on his own two feet and Edith, with her dispirited air, would never be other than a death's head at any feast.

'I'm looking for Kate – I thought she was talking to you!' Edith was at his elbow. Think of the devil, thought Samuel sourly.

'I see her, she's over there!' Edith had caught sight of Kate who had joined a group of friends on the lawn. She was quick on her pins, one had to say that for her, thought Samuel, surprised at the distance Kate had placed between them in such a short time.

'I want to make sure that she knows she's invited to lunch even though she's not on the committee any more. Shall I get Mrs Watson to take yours upstairs – or would you prefer it in the morning-room?'

'What? No, no, no need to bother about me – I had a biscuit with my coffee.'

'But you must have something!' Edith was concerned in case Samuel intended hanging around with a martyred air until one of the committee would jolly him into joining them in the dining-room. 'I know,' she said, her face clearing, 'why don't you take yourself along to The Cricketers?'

'Yes, I could do that – if it makes things easier for you.' They did a very decent mixed grill at The Cricketers on Thursdays which was something Samuel had remembered when he was soaking himself in the bath and to which he had been looking forward all morning.

'How did the "do" go off, then?' Dinner had been preceded by finishing off what had remained in the sherry decanter and such a civilised preliminary had encouraged Edward to make an effort at conversational exchage.

'Actually, I think it went rather well – didn't it, Samuel?'

But Samuel did not appear to have heard Edith. He was too absorbed in calculating which slice of quiche carried the greatest number of black olives. It was not often that the cuisine at Westwood excited much pleasurable deliberation, but tonight the table looked quite attractive – in a bitty sort of way. Edith, having profited from the experience of previous culinary disasters, had wisely purchased pâtés and quiches from the delicatessen. She had overestimated on the watercress and salad ingredients and, as it had not occurred to her to add a French dressing, the contents of the half-filled bowls were still both attractive and edible. Nor could the Stilton be faulted – although some philistine had elected to scoop right into it; but Samuel forebore to remark on the fact, generously conceding that women could not be expected to understand such niceties.

'Make a nice profit?' Edward asked, not really caring.

'Yes, I think so. Mrs Casement seemed quite happy with it. We're very lucky to have her as treasurer,' Edith added, wondering as soon as she had done so why one always felt it necessary to explain in some such fashion Mrs Casement's membership of the Winnies. After all, divorce was almost respectable nowadays; but the details could be unpalatable.

'What you putting the money to this year – not that damn-fool Youth Club again, I hope?' asked Samuel.

'No, no. Surely I told you that we're hoping to make a substantial donation this year to The Larches? They're very hard-pressed now, what with inflation and so forth, and a lot of the residents really cannot contribute more. Every little helps.'

'The Larches? That place for old loonies you mean – the Baxters' old property?'

Edith coloured a little with annoyance, but it was not unbecoming. After the committee had finally left, and with no preparations to be made for the evening meal, she had managed to take a little nap; that, and a sense of satisfaction now that the excitement of the day was behind her, had wiped her face clear of tension. She can still look really pretty when she tries, thought Edward, noting, too, that her voice had an edge of asperity as she answered Samuel.

'That's a very cruel, insensitive thing to say! The residents *are* elderly, past managing on their own, a little . . . confused. The Larches fills a great need. There's quite a waiting-list, you know.'

Samuel just grunted. He was well aware of the waiting-list and hoped it would continue to be long. There were times when he felt very uneasy about the proximity of The Larches and he was not sure that he approved of Edith's attention being drawn to its function.

'Mrs Casement has just managed to get her old aunt in – I think Matron was able to pull a few strings.'

'Her aunt – d'you mean Vicky?' The alarm in Samuel's voice was muted by a chunk of Stilton. He remembered Vicky clearly, much in demand for mixed doubles in the old days; a remarkable overhead smash. Hair the colour of butterscotch and hips as slender as a boy's.

'What they put Vicky away for?'

'It's not a case of anyone "putting her away" Samuel! She was jolly lucky to get in. Don't you remember that there was a bad break-in at her house last year – they got away with a lot of silver and a couple of very good Persian rugs? The police never caught whoever it was – I suppose it's the motorway being so near, they get away so quickly.' Edith was spreading Camembert thickly on a cracker, having decided that, it being so beautifully ripe, there would be no virtue in being frugal with it.

'Of course I remember!' Samuel sounded testy. 'Nothing wrong with my memory. But I don't see what that's got to do with her niece shoving her into The Larches.'

'But it's got a lot to do with it. The whole thing left the poor old girl very shaken. She got terribly nervous about being on her own – started to do silly absent-minded things too. You know, leaving the taps running, forgetting to light the gas – oh, all sorts of things. Worried Penny Casement terribly. She even set fire to an armchair one night, must have dropped a cigarette down the side and didn't even notice! It smouldered all night, Penny told me about it, a great wonder the house wasn't burned down. Anyway, I think it was the shock of that that made her Aunt Vicky see the sense of going in to The Larches. The family are very relieved. I think the Gas Board are buying the house – offices or something!' Edith turned to Felicity. 'Try some cheese, dear. It's really lovely.'

Felicity shook her head. She regretted now the tin of coke and the large wedge of Lily's fruitcake which had seemed such a good idea at the time.

'The increase in housebreaking these days is a crying disgrace! And the police seem powerless to do anything about it.' Samuel felt the conversation would benefit by a shift to the general from the particular. He had heard quite enough about The Larches and didn't want to brood on the fate of poor Vicky.

'Should never have put them in these damned cars – what d'you call 'em? Pandy things. What we need is the police-man back on the beat on his two feet. Wrote a letter to the *Telegraph* about it the other week. Ignored it, of course. Any-thing that stands to sense gets ignored these days. Next thing,

I shouldn't wonder, will be computers instead of Bobbies!'

'Oh, I nearly forgot!' Edith was pouring out the coffee from the silver pot which had been brought out and polished up for the luncheon party. It certainly gave an air to the table – perhaps she should make an effort and use Dora's silver more often, even if the cleaning of it was such a chore. Her hand on the coffeepot looked quite graceful, thought Edith; it was probably the nail polish, she decided – it improved the look of her hands, made the skin seem whiter. But, of course, it wasn't practical for everyday use. It was doing the vegetables that played such havoc – particularly scraping the early potatoes! She stirred her coffee dreamily.

'Well . . . what?' prompted Samuel, hoping it wouldn't be something more about The Larches.

'Lily Gudgeon!' Edith had come back to earth.

'What about her?' Edward had jerked his head up anxiously, remembering her telephone call of that morning and wondering if she had spoken in the same oblique, veiled terms to Edith.

'Well, she was here this morning, you see.' Edith waved a hand dismissively as Edward seemed inclined to interrupt.

'She always manages to find out the date somehow – well, I think I know how, but that's not what I wanted to tell you. Apparently she told Monica – she does the cake-stall, you know – that *she* had a robbery!' Edith paused, sensing that she had everyone's attention, and enjoying the novelty.

'Well – go on, Woman!' Samuel would have sounded more eager had it not been for the fact that Lily Gudgeon had appeared as smugly unruffled as ever that morning. She hadn't looked like a woman who had suffered a traumatic loss – unfortunately. But then one could never be sure with a woman like that.

'Well, it wasn't much really – perhaps she even made it up.' Edith regretted now her dramatic pause, feeling the story rather too lame to justify it.

'Just a cake and a sieve, actually. She *says* she had made this huge fruitcake to bring this morning' – come to think of it, Edith thought, that did sound unlikely. Although Lily *might* have done, in order to impress in some way. 'Well, she put the cake to cool on a sieve in front of her kitchen window and then when she went back later it had just . . . gone! That's what she said, anyway.'

'God bless my soul!' remarked Samuel, but then a happy thought struck him. 'Perhaps she imagined the whole thing. Never made a cake to be pinched, d'you see? Just going loopy – ripe for The Larches! Look here,' he added, turning quite excitedly towards Edward. 'If the old bat went funny, she'd *have* to get out of the cottage, wouldn't she? You know, get a doctor to certify – that sort of thing?'

Edward shrugged. 'Not as simple as that. Clearly Mrs Casement's aunt came herself to the conclusion that she would be well advised to give up her home and go into The Larches. There may have been an element of persuasion, *but*,' Edward continued in his dry, pedantic way, 'essentially it was a voluntary decision. If Lily ever came round to thinking along these lines, then one would hope that Edith could exert as much pull on her behalf with the matron as Mrs Casement seems to have done in the case of her aunt! But when it comes to the authorities intervening against a person's wishes – even if it is in the person's best interest – then things are very different. Complicated business, committal. Anyway there's nothing really to go on. Lily Gudgeon seems more in possession of her wits than most, if you ask me!'

Samuel glowered. Edward's last sentence had sounded, in some way, offensive. He wagged his cheese-smeared knife at his son.

'Sometimes I wonder just how keen you are to get that old bag out. Oh, it's all very well for you! You can afford to wait, but I'm sick and tired of being kept hanging about waiting to get back my own property before it's too late to have a bit of a fling!'

Why had she ever mentioned the wretched woman? Edith asked herself, miserably. Just when everything was going so nicely he has to start getting into one of his states again! And it's set his indigestion off, she thought, seeing the way Samuel suddenly caught his breath in anticipation of one of his coarse belches. Felicity had noticed it too, because she said, quickly:

'I'll get you your medicine, Grandfather. Probably the cheese – on top of all that work you must have done this morning!'

Edith smiled with grateful surprise as Felicity rose from the table. She'd put that really tactfully. They could surprise one quite agreeably at times, the young. Seemingly so wrapped up in their own affairs, but yet noticing more of what went on around them than they were often given credit for.

Felicity returned so swiftly, and handed him the glass of stomach mixture with such solicitude, that Samuel, mollified, decided not to pursue the matter of Lily Gudgeon further. In any case, he told himself, his eye alighting on the Stilton, it would be a pity to allow his digestion to be upset while such a sizable part of that round remained.

'Whatever you do – don't put it in the refrigerator!' he instructed Edith, with a nod in the direction of the cheese.

10

She couldn't ignore the noise – the sound made by the repeated slamming of the front-door knocker was too loud for that to be possible. But Lily could decline to heed it.

Lily Gudgeon had made herself so comfortable on the sofa that her reluctance to get up was understandable. Her ankles, a trifle swollen, rested on a cushion and her feet, clad only in donkey-brown support hose, rejoiced in their shoeless state. A second cushion had, by dint of much wriggling and prodding, been placed at the precise strategic angle to give maximum relief to her back. Her dentures, stridently pink and lemon against the white linen of her handkerchief, rested on her lap. Tea things stood on a small table at her side and included a plateful of scones still hot from the oven and flanked by a dish of butter and a bowl of raspberry jam.

Whoever it was who stood there, rat-tat-tatting, was certainly persistent, thought Lily, spooning jam on to a scone saturated with melting butter. The radio, being turned on, made it obvious that she was at home. It couldn't be Miss Sinclair, she decided, this not being a Wednesday which was her early-closing day. Besides, Miss Sinclair knew better than to call unannounced, Lily having made it very clear that she disliked the custom of casual popping-in. It might be the Mormons back again – but surely that was scarcely likely, considering how she'd sent them away with a flea in their ear the last time they'd ventured to call? The meter reader? Parcel post?

Unable to relax in the manner to which she felt entitled while her mind was so teased with speculation and her ears so assaulted with noise, Lily swilled a mouthful of tea round her gums to wash away any raspberry seeds that clung, and thrust her false teeth back in position.

Felicity had been on the point of giving up and going away when the door jerked open. Now she almost wished that she had come to that decision a fraction sooner. Seen at such close quarters and viewed from the lowest of the three steps leading down from the door, Lily was a more formidable figure than Felicity had quite bargained for. She looked very large, very red in the face and very cross.

'I am sorry to disturb you, Mrs Gudgeon.' Felicity, her eyes wide and innocent, injected into her modulated voice a discreet tone of deference. The effect of this effort seemed wasted on Lily who, after the initial surprise of finding the Gordon-Fenn child on her doorstep, had eyes only for what Felicity held in her hands.

'What are you doing with my sieve?' she asked, bluntly.

'Oh, it *is* yours – I'm so glad. I was sure it must be, after what Mummy said.'

'Of course it's mine! I'd know it anywhere; you can't get them like that nowadays – not hair sieves.' Lily was stretching out a hand for her property, but Felicity affected not to notice it.

'I expect you're wondering how I got it? But I'm jolly glad it was found – it must be quite valuable, really, almost a sort of antique!'

Good gracious! I do believe the child is expecting some sort of reward, thought Lily, admitting to herself a wry satisfaction in the prospect of handing out a tip to Samuel's grand-daughter. Felicity certainly didn't look like a child who would be over-indulged where pocket money was concerned. Her clothes looked positively poverty-stricken, Lily noted, taking a closer look at the girl. Her blue and white checked gingham had the faded, shrunken look of a dress that had been to the wash more often than was reasonable and a band of wide blue ribbon had been clumsily inserted above the hem by way of lengthening the skirt; her plimsolls were shabby and the toes of both had been roughly darned.

Felicity bore Lily's overt appraisal with modestly down-cast eyes and inner satisfaction. She had been almost over-whelmed by choice when it had come to selecting clothes which would evoke sympathy, but it was good to know that the time spent in preparation had not been wasted. The darns on the toes of last year's plimsolls had been an inspired touch of artistry, mere holes might have given an appearance of slovenly carelessness, but the darns carried a far more poignant significance.

'Hold on a minute,' said Lily, as she left the front door to fetch her purse.

She was a little startled as she turned from the kitchen with her purse in her hand to find Felicity standing in the middle of her sitting-room.

'Oh, I say! You did mean me to come in – didn't you?' Felicity's tone was still respectful but there was something about her cultured accent that reminded Lily that Felicity belonged to a family which was not accustomed to being kept hanging about on doorsteps.

Well, she might momentarily have been put at a disad-vantage, but Lily had no intention of remaining at one.

'Here!' she said, taking a couple of ten-pence pieces from her purse and holding them out to Felicity. 'Take this as a little reward for bringing back my property.'

Felicity, with every appearance of shocked embarrassment, shook her head vigorously. 'Oh no, Mrs Gudgeon – I couldn't possibly!' She put her hands, empty now as she had put the sieve down on the chenille-covered table, firmly behind her back to emphasise her refusal.

'Don't be silly!' said Lily, advancing with the intention of pushing the coins into the pocket of Felicity's dress.

Felicity, still shaking her head, backed away. She narrowly missed colliding with the little table by the sofa and, finally, as it caught the back of her knees she fell abruptly into the chair which (not quite by chance) had been in the direct line of her retreat.

Lily, to her own annoyance, felt distinctly awkward, if

not downright crass, standing over this embarrassed girl who seemed to be almost cowering in the armchair as though overwhelmed by the sheer vulgarity of the situation. There was something about the way in which Felicity was now avoiding her eye that implied that her evident embarrassment was more for Lily than herself.

'Well, if you're sure . . .' Lily dropped the coins back into her purse, which she closed with a little snap. 'It was just that I thought . . . well – '

'Oh please, Mrs Gudgeon, don't think any more about it! I'm sure you didn't mean to . . . well, anyway, don't worry about it!' Felicity was quite pink, as though covered in confusion in her eagerness to forgive Lily for her gaffe. 'Would you like me to tell you about the sieve – how I came to find it, you know?' she asked in a rush, as though anxious to give Lily time to recover from her gaucherie.

'But perhaps,' she added, glancing at the tea tray, 'you'd really rather I leave you in peace to get on with your tea!'

Lily, not quite understanding how it was that she now found herself in the role of potential hostess, insisted that Felicity remain and share her tea and the scones.

Felicity proved to have an excellent appetite and despatched a remarkable quantity of scones but with such flattering praise of Lily's baking that, at the time, Lily felt rather gratified and it seemed almost a privilege to ply her young visitor with gingerbread and currant cake fetched from their tins in the larder. It was only when Felicity had left that Lily experienced both a sense of wonder and a pang of regret over how much of the raspberry jam had disappeared, particularly as – it being out of the question in the circumstances for her to have taken out her tiresome dentures – she had been unable to eat any of it herself. It had been the last of her supply and there would be no more until Westwood's tangled thicket of canes ripened their current crop. But the regret was brief and not dwelt upon because, by then, Lily had other things to mull over.

Felicity had related how, the previous Saturday afternoon,

she had seen a youth (a rough, loutish-looking fellow) running across the orchard as though he had come from the direction of Lily's cottage. Felicity had been so scared at the sudden appearance of such a dangerous-looking trespasser that her first reaction, as she rather shamefacedly confessed, had been to hide herself behind some bushes. But, fortunately, he had not seen her and, peeping through the branches, Felicity had seen him veer away towards the sloping ground that ran down towards the motorway. Just before he had become hidden by the thicket that covered the place where once the wood had stood, she had got a brief impression of him throwing something away. But, of course, he had then been quite a distance away and she could have been mistaken. And yes, looking back on it, Felicity was almost sure that he had had something hidden under his anorak which might well have been a cake; the bulge had had a roundish shape, she remembered that because at the time she had imagined it to be a crash helmet as he had had the look of the sort of hooligan one thought of as tearing around on a motorbike. It was only, Felicity had said, after her mother had recounted the story of the theft of Lily's cake and the sieve that Felicity had begun to wonder if there could have been any connexion. Since then, Felicity had said, she had spent quite a lot of time searching around the spot where she calculated the boy had been when he had seemed to throw something away. She had almost given up the search when she had eventually spotted the sieve far below her – being round, as she had reasonably pointed out, it had rolled quite a distance.

No, Felicity had replied to Lily's query, she had not told her mother about her find. She hadn't wanted to alarm her mother by letting her know that a burglar seemed to know his way around the grounds of Westwood. Her mother, as Felicity explained, was already terrified by the thought of intruders. There had been such a wave of burglaries recently in the neighbourhood. Mrs Casement's poor old aunt had never really got over the burglary at her home. Felicity had gone on to describe just how the shock had affected the unfortunate woman. Lily, who had a great appetite for news of the misfortunes of others, had listened with interest and, by dint of probing, had extracted from Felicity references to several other distressing cases despite Felicity's apparent reluctance to pursue the subject. Eventually Felicity said, but in a polite and diffident way, that she really should not be repeating all these things and that her father would be very cross if he were ever to learn that she had been re-counting things which she had heard discussed at home. Her father, of course, heard various things from the police in the way that a solicitor would. But Lily assured Felicity that there was no need to fear that she had repeated anything which she should not have done as Lily recollected having read in the local paper reports of the incidents which Felicity had confided. That had seemed to relieve Felicity of any fears that she had been indiscreet – at least she had smiled very delightfully.

It was little wonder, Lily reflected, that Edward Gordon-Fenn did not appear to have much success in his profession, lacking, as he obviously did, even the basic requirement of discretion! The man was clearly a fool and it was very grati-fying to have confirmation of her intuitive opinion. The child, of course, had had no notion of the implications of what she had so innocently repeated. Mrs Casement, with her hoity-toity airs, would certainly not want it known that her aunt had actually been attacked in a very nasty way by one of the louts who had burgled her house. Felicity had been vague about the details – but then that was only natural because, as Lily had to admit to herself (reluctant though she was to accord any virtue to the Gordon-Fenns), Felicity was clearly a well-brought-up child with the commendable innocence that that condition conferred.

Lily, who always found an acknowledgement of pleasure a difficult admission to make even to herself, had really en-joyed Felicity's unexpected visit. The fact that she had no contact with the young did not deter Lily from holding very strong opinions on the younger generation, but she was persuaded that Felicity, so polite, so demure, was clearly the exception that proved the rule. Felicity had shown a nice concern, too, when Lily, rising to take the teapot to the kitchen for a refill, had out of habit clapped her hand to her back. When Lily, glad of the rare opportunity of complaining to a receptive listener, had told Felicity about the lumbago that plagued her back and the rheumatism which was lodged in her knee, Felicity had expressed a wish to be allowed to help in some way. Perhaps, she had suggested, she could assist with the shopping sometimes – or mow the lawn; but then she had checked herself and, with the open candour which one finds so appealing in the young and so embarrassing in the mature, had stated that if Lily didn't want her help she had only to say so! Lily had not been so disarmed as to abandon an ingrained habit of wariness, but, while not accepting Felicity's offer of help, had said it would be nice if she could look in again some time.

Lily had suggested to Felicity that she leave by the back door as the route home was obviously shorter through the garden than by the road.

As Lily reached up for the key which hung on a hook by the back door, she confided to Felicity that ever since the theft of her cake she had kept the doors locked even during the day and was careful never to leave a window open in an unoccupied room. Felicity had agreed that such precautions were wise but had added that she did hope all her chatter about burglaries would not make Lily worry about it. Living on one's own could make one worry far too much about such things and it would be such a pity if Lily let it distress her because it just wasn't worth it. After all, as Felicity pointed out with an encouraging smile and a voice full of determined brightness, there had probably been nothing more behind the theft of the cake than a nasty boy's greed. He had probably just smelt the cake in passing and had succumbed to sudden temptation. Quite an old head on young shoulders, thought Lily indulgently, remembering the phrase having been used in relation to herself many years ago. If, in her own case, there had been pejorative under-tones in the description, she preferred not to consider them.

Lily stood by the open door for a minute watching Felicity skipping across her lawn with an almost conscious gaiety, as though she were determined to leave Lily feeling happy and reassured! At the gate in the garden wall, Felicity paused for a moment to turn and wave cheerily to Lily before letting it creak noisily shut behind her. I must oil it, thought Felicity, the happy smile still on her lips.

But how, thought Lily, as she hung the key back on its hook, had that boy managed to smell the cake if he had not already been trespassing in her garden? The smell would hardly have travelled to the road in front of the cottage even allowing for the fact that the best part of a bottle of stout had gone into her cake. No, she rebuked herself. I won't allow myself to worry about it. The child was quite right when she advised me not to think about it. After all, look at the state to which pointless worry brought that other poor woman, whatever her name was . . . that Mrs Casement's old aunt! Getting muddled, forgetting things. But then she was probably going dotty anyway – that class of person often did – only they called it 'becoming a little eccentric'. They had life too easy, that was why their brains rotted in age, the wages of indolent youth and over-indulgence in life's luxuries. Well, thought Lily self-righteously, no one could accuse me of having led an inactive youth! I always had to carry more than my fair share. Put-upon, that's what I was. I'll just check that I did turn off the gas taps tightly, not that I ever do forget to do that sort of thing, Lily told herself, but when one has a visitor one can become distracted – however careful one is normally.

11

Felicity found that climbing out of the window of the old laundry-room was quite easy, even in the dark. Had there been a bulb in the socket of the dangling flex in the middle of the room she could not have benefited from its use as, the sole switch being by the door, the light would have had to be left on until her return. Above the deep sinks in front of the window there ran a wide, tiled ledge within easy stepping distance from the top of the copper wash-boiler. Once through the window, a gnarled thick stem of ivy afforded a convenient hand- and toe-hold on the short drop to the ground below.

The first few of Felicity's night exits had been effected more conventionally by way of the back door. But one night Samuel, on a late kitchen prowl in search of a little something to take the edge off his appetite, had discovered that the bolt on the back door was drawn and the key unturned. He had remedied these omissions and it was on that night, finding herself locked out, that Felicity had had recourse to the window of the disused laundry; a window which, as she had discovered to her relief, had a rusted and broken catch. Samuel had made a great fuss at breakfast the following morning about the unlocked door and the feckless irresponsibility that that revealed. They might, he had declared, have all been murdered in their beds and without even the comfort of insurance compensation as there would clearly have been contributory negligence on the part of the victims – or at least on the part of *one*, he had amended, glaring at Edith. Edith had protested that she was positive that she had locked up after letting Puss-puss out for the night. Edith had noticed that Puss-puss had of late shown a preference for spending his nights in the garden and she had begun to suspect that what he sought there was respite from the activities of the mice indoors; but, with Samuel already looking so irate, she had felt that this was not the best moment to voice her anxieties on that score. If she was so sure that she had let Puss-puss out, how was it then – Samuel had asked with all the triumphant sarcasm of a prosecuting counsel – that he had discovered Puss-puss not only very much in the kitchen but, in fact, sitting on the table licking the cream out of the very bit of sponge cake which Samuel himself had hoped to find in the cake tin? Felicity sat silent, alarmed and cross with herself for being so careless. But she need not have worried, as no breath of suspicion fell upon her. Edith was puzzled about the sponge cake as she had been equally certain that the last of the cake had been put away in its tin before she had left the kitchen. But if, as it now seemed, she had let Puss-puss in and not out, then she really could not insist on the accuracy of her memory. Edith had admitted culpability with as good a grace as she could assume, the humiliation being tempered by the belief that she was setting a good example to Felicity in respect of being prepared to admit when one was in the wrong.

Once accustomed to it, Felicity experienced a pleasant sense of adventure in using the unorthodox route of exit and entry provided by the window. Out of fear of mislaying it, or indeed of it being discovered in her room, Felicity always returned the spare key of the cottage to where she had first found it – which was hanging with other long-unused keys on a board in the laundry-room. Thus, even before she had thought of using the window rather than the back door, Felicity had already acquainted herself with the old laundry-room and, by virtue of familiarity, had learned to disregard its less agreeable features. She had learned, for instance, that the cockroaches, which the vibrations of her approaching feet sent scurrying across the damp, flagged floor, possessed no inclination to clamber up her legs. The mice, their senses finely tuned by the awareness that they shared their territory with a cat (even one as lax and peace-loving as Puss-puss), streaked so quickly out of sight that one was scarcely aware of their presence. But Felicity did know that they were there and so was not at all alarmed by a quick flicker of movement caught, briefly, in the beam of her torch. She knew, too, where the spiders hung their webs and so ran no risk of brushing into them and finding a dispossessed weaver crawling across her face. The coffin in the corner had lost its power to strike its beholder with terror. It had only been that first glimpse by night that had evoked in Felicity a frisson of fear. Seen in daylight it had never deceived. Felicity had known that it was nothing more than a worm-eaten box that housed a croquet set; the black coffin shape of its lid only a crude optical illusion. A ghoulish joke perpetrated with black paint in the long ago by one of her grandmother Edwina's rackety friends.

Outside, on the ground below the window, Felicity stood quite still for a couple of minutes while her eyes became accustomed to the darkness. The torch which, along with the heavy old-fashioned key weighted down her pocket, was not for use in the garden. One never knew who might, in sleepless mood, be moved to look out from the blank windows of the upstairs rooms. The rank smell of crushed ivy and trampled Bishop's weed filled her nostrils. Her ears picked up the tiny noises of night, the little sounds that pass unnoticed in the lively hours of daylight: the whisper of a falling leaf, the creak of a branch, a rustle in the undergrowth as some nocturnal creature crept on its way, or a bird, disturbed by the soft thud as her feet had touched the ground, resettled on its roost.

Her pale hair hidden by the hood of her dark gaberdine raincoat, Felicity set off through the garden: a moving shadow weaving between the black, still shapes of shrubs and hedges and melting into the darkness below the overcast night sky.

The sweet, fresh smell of new-mown grass hung in the air above Lily's little lawn. Felicity noted it with approval.

Handicapped as she was by rheumatism, Lily's movements were never swift but now, after exertion in the garden, the risk of her getting downstairs quickly enough to apprehend an intruder was even slighter than usual. Besides, Lily generally slept sound and deep, a happy circumstance indeed, which, as she had confided to Felicity, was entirely due to her sleeping pills which the doctor so understandingly and liberally prescribed.

Once inside the cottage, Felicity slipped back the hood of her coat. Lily, whose pale eyes had, as Felicity had observed, a certain lizard-like quality, was very fond of warmth and even in summer time kept a fire burning in her living-room. The fire had been carefully damped down for the night and the hearth swept and tidied. Although the room was so warm, the cushions so plump and numerous, the shelves and mantelpiece so cluttered with knick-knacks, the atmosphere was not one of drowsy comfort. Every object and feature in the room upon which a shine could be inflicted gleamed and shone with sharp, cold intensity. The wooden floor surround, the cream paintwork, the willow-pattern plates upon the walls, the old-fashioned brass fender and coal scuttle, the glass and china ornaments and even the dark leaves of the sullen plant in the copper trough upon the window ledge – all glittered with a restless, glacial brilliance. As Felicity swept the light of her torch over the room, scores of glittering eyes seemed to wink and blink briefly in the glancing beam.

Lily's knitting lay, neatly rolled, on the sofa. Felicity took one of the needles and placed it in the brass cylinder on the hearth which held the poker; the poker itself she rolled up in the knitting. Miss Frobisher often said that it was the little things that counted and that 'great oaks from little acorns grow', thought Felicity, wiping her hands clean of the soot from the poker with her handkerchief before turning on the television set and adjusting the volume so that the warning sound would not carry upstairs.

It was Sally who had, unwittingly, given her the idea

about the television set. She had arrived late for school, bursting with the importance of the drama she could scarcely wait to tell. The road near her home had been blocked with fire engines, hoses, police cars and a crowd of onlookers outside the house of an elderly lady who lived alone and whose downstairs rooms had been quite badly damaged by fire. Sally had gabbled on a great deal about the damage caused, perhaps sensing that the fact that the old lady herself had escaped unscathed would end the story on a disappointing note of anti-climax. But, according to Sally, she and her mother had heard one of the firemen give it as his opinion that the fire had been started by a television set left on overnight. There had been a photographer there from the local paper, so it would be bound to be reported in Friday's edition.

Having done what she had come to do, Felicity indulged herself by standing for a few minutes in the little hall, feasting her eyes on what was kept in the glass-fronted cabinet that stood there. It was a matter of irritation that Lily kept its doors locked and that Felicity on her several night time visits had, as yet, failed to find the key. They had belonged to her mother, Lily had said, the nine little china cottages. There had once been ten but one had been broken by the removal men. No, Lily could not remember what it had looked like, the cottage whose careless loss seemed so to shock her visitor. It had not seemed to occur to Lily to unlock the doors and although Felicity longed to hold the cottages in her hands, she had not asked to be allowed to do so, being ever conscious of the need to be polite and not in any way to 'take liberties', as Lily herself would have put it. But now that she knows me better, thought Felicity giving the glass a rub where her breath had clouded it, perhaps I could ask her the next time she offers to let me look at them – and then I'll see where she keeps the key.

There was something so enchanting, so safe, so lovable about the little cottages that every time Felicity looked at them she felt a sensation, somewhere at the back of her nose, as though she wanted to cry. Not sad tears, she thought, trying to find reason in her desire to invite such strange disquiet, but the sort of tears that she sometimes found cool upon her cheeks when she wakened from a dream. It was a dream which, once awake, she could never remember but which she knew had been so beautiful that it could have had nothing to do with real life.

Standing there, with her back to the dark stairway, Felicity felt a chilly sensation behind her; almost as though she was being watched from somewhere up there, outside Lily's bedroom. It was only the draught from the open bathroom window, she told herself, it blew under the door and down the narrow canyon of the stairs. Felicity had never ventured upstairs by night, that would be foolish; but she had, on the pretext of using the lavatory, been up there in the daytime. Lily had stood waiting for her at the bottom of the stairs but Felicity had glimpsed enough to know that Lily's bedroom lay to the left, another room (the door of which had been closed) was on the right and the bathroom was straight ahead.

Felicity stared upwards now. Nothing stirred, no shape darker than the surrounding gloom stood at the top of the stairs.

She pulled her hood up over her head and left as silently as she had come, pausing only to lift the empty milk bottle from the back doorstep and place it in the sink before turning her key in the lock behind her. The key turned with quiet ease, the lock having responded as gratefully as had the hinges of the iron gate to the attention she had given them with the oil-can on the first of her nocturnal visits.

'Well, I must say that was very thoughtful of you!' Lily took the handful of magazines from Felicity and laid them on the grass beside her deck-chair.

The day was very warm and the air filled with that oppressive, heavy stillness that precedes a thunderstorm. Felicity had been relieved to discover that Lily was sitting out in the garden as she had noticed that, even on a day such as this, a thin plume of smoke rose from the cottage chimney. But Lily was taking no chances with the vagaries of the weather, and wore a puce-coloured cardigan over her pink dress to guard against chill, and a rayon scarf of much the same shade sheltered her head from the rays of the sun. It might have been wiser to have worn a brimmed hat as her face had been caught by the sun and the shiny red blotches on cheeks and nose went ill with the colour above and below.

'I really enjoyed that last lot you brought – you know, these old *Reader's Digests*. Really good, they were!'

'I think I can find you some more.' Felicity knew that she could. There was quite a pile of back numbers stowed away in the tennis pavilion. Samuel gave her little batches from time to time to take to the Old Sailors' Home – but that was rather a long walk away. Samuel set great store by the magazine, saying that it kept a busy man like himself up-to-date on a wide variety of topics and dispensed with the need for a great deal of tedious reading. He particularly liked the potted versions of books as he believed that an educated man had a responsibility to keep himself informed as to the literary works of his time and these admirable summaries 'cut the cackle and got down to the essentials' as he described it.

It was not only in choice of reading matter that Samuel's and Lily's opinions agreed. Felicity had learned that, unlikely as it seemed, these sworn enemies really held many views in common. It was puzzling, but very convenient. Felicity had only to repeat one of her grandfather's opinions in order to gain Lily's instant respect and agreement. Naturally, she realised that it would be unwise to reveal that these views were those of Samuel and so she attributed them to her mother. Lily had, in the past, had a poor opinion of Edith but now she freely admitted to herself that she had been doing that lady a gross injustice. She was now doing her best to make up for it and only that week had smiled most affably at Edith in the supermarket and had even helpfully drawn her attention to a Special Offer of soft tomatoes. Mrs Gordon-Fenn had appeared suitably overwhelmed.

'Have a sweetie, dear. There's a box of marshmallows in my workbag – I put it under my chair to keep it out of the sun.'

Felicity obediently hauled the workbag from under Lily's deck-chair. The bulge of Lily's bottom had rather compressed the contents of the bag and the sweets were both squashed and unpleasantly warm. But Felicity was not obliged to have her politeness put under too much stress because, having once proffered the box, Lily thereafter kept it on her lap where she absent-mindedly dipped into it from time to time until it soon held nothing but a dusting of loose sugar which she gathered up on a moist finger.

'Would you like your knitting?' asked Felicity, helpfully shaking out the acid-green roll wrapped round the steel needles.

'Not just now. It's too hot.'

'Oh dear!' Felicity exclaimed, rolling the work up again, 'what a nasty dirty mark across it – however did that happen?'

'I don't know,' Lily mumbled indistinctly, but truthfully, round a wodge of marshmallows. 'Something foolish I did without thinking.'

That was one of the nice things about Felicity, thought Lily, she was cheerful and never pried or asked questions.

Felicity was pushing the knitting back into the bag and had come across the local paper which she began to smooth and shake into orderly shape.

'Don't bother with that – I've finished with it.'

'Wasn't it awful about that fire – you know, the story on the front page with the photograph? Fancy anyone leaving a television on all night! But I suppose the poor old lady has just grown absent-minded; so dangerous when she lives on her own.'

Instead of replying, Lily tossed the now empty sweet box

to Felicity and asked her to run and put it and the newspaper in the bin by the back door. 'And I'll go and get us a
drink of lemonade,' she added, heaving herself about in the
chair.

'No, don't move! I can bring it, if you tell me where to
find things – that is,' Felicity added shyly, 'if you don't mind
letting me in your kitchen.'

Lily explained to Felicity just where to find the glasses and
lemonade and which tins in the larder held biscuits and which
held cakes. She had to repeat the instructions, but did so
patiently as on Felicity's previous visits Lily had refused her
offers of help, so it was only to be expected that the arrangement of the kitchen was a mystery to her.

When Felicity had run happily to the kitchen, Lily watching the girl's light, blithe movement with a certain pang of
envy, thought how surprising it was that she had so quickly
got on such easy, friendly terms with one of the Gordon-
Fenns. Surprising, really, that she had arrived at any sort
of relationship that was not purely acrimonious, never mind
the time span! 'It only goes to show – ' Lily told herself, but
was uncertain just what was demonstrated. Perhaps, she
reflected, it has something to do with growing old. Not that
one liked to think that one was growing old, but at seventy-
two one had to face facts and lately, what with her rheumatism and one thing and another (here Lily's mind skidded
swiftly over some nasty bumps) she had had the reality of
her age forced upon her consciousness. Age did mellow one,
blunt the edges of one's sharper reactions; made one a trifle
less intolerant, or so it was said. Not, Lily told herself, that
she could ever come not to hate Samuel! Not even if I
should live to be a hundred, she thought, and then consciously
checked the feeling of wrath that rose within her whenever
she allowed her mind to dwell on that man. Feelings of
anger are very bad for my blood pressure, she reminded
herself; goodness knows how that vile man has undermined
my health over the years! The extraordinary thing is that
he should have such a pleasant grand-daughter – he certainly

doesn't deserve her. His son is a milksop. But then, perhaps Edward was not his son at all – that would scarcely be surprising, thought Lily with an involuntary little smile. The smile, which had been rather disagreeable in the first place, lingered, and Lily became aware that her lips were unpleasantly parched and sticky and hoped that Felicity would not be too long in bringing the lemonade.

Ah, there she was now! Not running any more, but walking carefully so as not to jog the tray she carried, her eyes on the brimming glasses, her expression serious. Lily, quite forgetting the inadvisability of it, smiled again, but this time it was an indulgent, almost fond smile, so its lingering nature was not too unpleasant. The sight of it certainly gave Felicity satisfaction.

'I was thinking quite a lot about when I was young,' said Lily when half her lemonade had gone in one glorious thirst-quenching gulp.

'Did I ever tell you that I was in the ATS in the war? A sergeant, no less – I expect that surprises you!' It surprised Lily herself sometimes when she looked back upon it. At times it seemed like yesterday, the war; other times it seemed to have belonged to a very distant bygone age. But it was comforting, when one was visited with disquieting doubts as to one's capabilities, to remember the days when one had been both efficient and in authority. When everything about one had been . . . what was it one used to say? . . . yes, that was it, 'tickety-boo'!

Felicity's expression was politely attentive, but she hoped she would not have to hold it for too long. Lily seemed to have dropped into a reverie. Her eyes had taken on a far-away look in much the same way as did Edith's when she shut herself away inside her head. But it was not easy to judge the expression in Lily's eyes at the best of times, so embedded were they between the swollen thickness of upper and lower lids; now these lids had almost completely closed – like the shells of a beached mussel. Perhaps, thought Felicity, on a note of hope, she's dropped off to sleep.

133

Lily, however, began to stir into activity. The deck-chair creaked as she heaved herself sideways and retrieved her workbag from the ground. She began to claw about inside it, letting her broad knobbly hands do the searching. The sides of the chintz bag undulated and bulged as though they imprisoned a frantic burrowing animal.

'I know I have it here somewhere!' Lily muttered, 'came across it the other day when I was tidying the bureau. Ah – ' she said, her eyes at last acknowledging her hands and looking down with approval at what they held.

The small brown paper wallet, limp and blotched with age, which Lily was so eagerly opening, looked unpromising. Felicity could see that it held a few photographs and negatives and she felt the slight interest aroused by Lily's enthusiastic search drain away.

'Come here – look at this!' Lily's tone was quite peremptory, as though recall of bygone glories had gone to her head.

Felicity, who had been growing a little tired of sitting on the grass in a demure but uncomfortable position, was quite glad to obey the command. Lily was holding up a photograph for admiration.

'That's me – the one with the sergeant's stripes!'

Of the group of grinning girls dressed in short, tight skirts and buttoned tunics, only one, the plump, grim-faced young woman perched on the tailboard of the truck round which the others were clustered, could possibly have been Lily. Even without the identification of the stripes, recognition was not difficult.

'You look very . . . serious,' said Felicity, feeling that some comment was awaited and glad that, standing as she was behind Lily's deck-chair, she had not needed to suppress her smile. How very odd they all looked! And Lily, with her fat thighs straining at her skirt and her clumsy cap dead straight on her head, looked the funniest of all!

'Well, it's a serious business, my girl – war! Of course I was older than a lot of the girls and more aware of the

responsibilities. A right handful they were, some of them –
but I soon sorted them out, I can tell you!'

'Did you like it – being in the Army, I mean?'

'Wasn't a case of liking or not liking. Doing one's duty,
that's what it was about.'

Lily had liked it. Had liked it very much. The war had
presented her with the opportunity of escape. Escape from
helping her father run the newsagent's shop; escape from the
cramped, stuffy little flat above the business, the rooms that
were filled with the sickly smell of chronic illness, sweet-
scented talcum powder and surgical spirit. Only at night
would Lily's mother permit the windows to be opened;
during the day they were shut tight against the fumes and the
noise of the traffic. The downstairs shop, in contrast, was
full of air; dust-laden and vitiated, but moving; gusting in
ahead of the customers through the door that stood exactly
on the corner where one street cut across the other. Early
winter mornings had been the worst; sorting the papers with
print-blackened hands, fingers stiff with cold, sleep-heavy
eyes smarting in the glare of the unshaded light. The paper
boys stamping their feet and blowing noisily into red, cupped
hands, the sharp cold smell of the night air that clung to
their clothes all too soon dissipated by the fumes of the newly-
lit paraffin stove and the smell of boiling porridge that crept
down the stairs.

'It's in the news a lot these days. There's a fancy name for
it – can't remember rightly what they call it – but they've
got their own Society and everything!'

'The Army?' asked Felicity, puzzled.

'No, no. What was wrong with my mother – creeping
paralysis we called it in our day. I don't suppose it matters
much what name you call it. All comes to the same-
thing.'

Felicity had heard all about the bedridden mother, or at
least the effect her disability had had on Lily's life. 'Nothing
better than an unpaid skivvy, I was. Even when I was still
at school, keeping things going, helping out all the time.

Some people don't know they're born!' That was how Lily had bitterly summed it up.

'How did your father manage then – when you went away in the war?'

'Well, Mother had passed on by then. Same time as Munich she went. Could have gone any time, but that's when it happened. Awful, it was – everyone crowding in for papers and Dad all gone to pieces. We put up the "Closed" card on the door but it made not a mite of difference, they still hammered away. You see, it was different in those days – no telly, so newspapers counted for something. But when the war came the shop slackened off – nothing much to sell, you see. Sweets on ration, cigarettes under the counter. All that. Dad managed on his own all right, not that much left to manage anyway!'

A shot rang out from the direction of Westwood, heavy and dull on the still, hot air.

'Murderer!' Lily muttered, but without fervour, her attention being on another photograph which she had slid from the wallet.

'Wedding day,' she said, cryptically, handing the shining snapshot over her shoulder to Felicity.

Lily, still in uniform, smiling stiffly, weighing down the arm of a slim figure in clumsy battledress. They stood in front of what, judging by the network of down-pipes and drains, must have been the back of a tall, narrow building. It was not what one could call a romantic setting, but there was nothing to suggest that the front of such a building would have afforded a more picturesque backdrop.

'The guests,' said Lily, producing another photograph. 'Dad's not in it, seeing as how he took the snap. But Mrs Gudgeon's there. I can't pick her out without my specs, but she's the one without a hat – the reception being in her own home. I couldn't put a name to most of them. They were her lodgers, you see – had to have them there seeing as how she'd pooled all their rations to put on a bit of a "do". She did herself well, that one – I can tell you! That lot never saw their butter ration: marg, that's what she kept them on. Always out for number one, she was! Her being a widow' (in fact, Lily harboured private reservations about the truth of that), 'and with only the one son, she just used him. Yes, the both of us had that in common, me and my husband; sometimes I think that's what brought us together really, a common bond, you might say. They didn't like it one little bit, you know – my father and his mother; us flying the nest like that when they thought they'd got us in their clutches for ever!'

What had Lily meant by 'same time as Munich', Felicity wondered. She had not asked Lily, as she sensed that this was going to be one of the days when she went drearily on and on and the best thing to do was to let her continue without interruption until she ran herself dry. It was extraordinary how Lily loved to talk about how awful the past had been for her, thought Felicity, angry about it but angrier still that not everybody had had such a miserable life. But perhaps she really needed to keep telling herself how dreadful it had all been so that the present, by contrast, seemed nicer than it could possibly be considered to be.

Felicity leaned forward and replaced the photographs, smudged now with the thumbprints left by Lily's damp hands, on Lily's ample lap. Lily replaced them in the wallet, but absent-mindedly, as though they had become an irrelevance once they had performed their function in stimulating memory. Once her feet had been guided to the path that led back to the past, Lily needed no further prod to keep her plodding along it.

It struck Felicity that Grandfather's use of his past was very different. Everything in Samuel's past was bathed in a rosy glow and his anger was directed at other people who were now, in his opinion, 'living the life of Riley'. It was all such a waste of time, thought Felicity impatiently, bothering about what other people had or didn't have. What one had to do was just decide what one wanted for oneself and then work hard at getting it – even if it meant enduring such boredom that her throat actually ached with the pent-up desire to scream and scream. But it would all be worth it in the end!

Lily, reflected Felicity, had never drawn her attention to that other photograph; but, as it was not tucked away in a drawer, forgotten, it must mean more to Lily than those that she had just resurrected and displayed. Felicity was thinking about the photograph which stood, in a silver frame, on the mantelshelf and which she had examined at her leisure by the light of her torch. That photograph looked as though it had been taken in a public garden: there was a formal bed of flowers in the background overhung by a grey, speckled tissue of blurred mist suggesting the presence of a sprinkler whose action had defeated the lens of the old-fashioned camera. But the figures in the foreground were well focused, clear and heartbreakingly distinct. It could not be on account of the unflattering likeness of herself that Lily gave the photograph such pride of place. Lily stood by a wheelchair, a lumpish child in a too-long dress ('to allow for growth,' Felicity had thought, recognising the signs of that adult, insensitive prudence with a certain sympathy). The face of the woman in the chair was pretty in a sad, wistful way. Her legs were shockingly thin, like a bird's, straight and with no plumpness at the calf whatsoever – as though the muscles had long wasted away from disuse. Lily's childhood face was only half visible as her head was turned towards the woman in the chair. She held one of the invalid's hands in her own. A mother holding the hand of her child in comfort and reassurance. But there was something disturbingly wrong in what the photograph portrayed. Felicity had been replacing it on the mantelshelf before it struck her that the photograph revealed that the woman in the wheelchair was the child and Lily the mother. She had picked it up again and had looked at it long, this sad testament of a truth that nudged one's sympathies from down the years. Lily really had had a dreadful life (just looking as ugly as she apparently had done apart from all the nasty things that had happened to her); it was little wonder that she had become such a repulsive person! Felicity felt a pang of guilt when she thought of what she was doing to the ill-used Lily Gudgeon. It did seem unfair that the crueller life was to one, then the more horrid one was likely to become and the more likely one was to attract dislike and abuse. But Lily, and Grandfather, too, for that matter, spat back at life, tearing with unsheathed claws. Felicity was conscious of a grudging admiration.

Seen from above, Lily's hair was noticeably thin on top, her scalp showed through, pink like a baby's. One never thought of old ladies going bald, only men. It must be rotten, growing old and being all filled up with sour memories and having lots of time to dwell on them; turning them over and over like onions in a jar full of vinegar. I'm not going to think about it, Felicity told herself, a shiver of premonition fleetingly touching her spine and chilling her sweat-damp flesh.

I'm doing Lily a good turn, really, Felicity assured herself. She'll be far happier in a Home with lots of people to talk to and quarrel with! Mummy will probably be able to get her in at The Larches (the Winnies can do things like that), and once she's there I'll visit her and bring her Grandfather's old magazines – sweets, too, because I'm bound to get more pocket-money once we're rich. It's not as though I'll have to go too often . . . once a month perhaps. It won't be too awful because once she has other people to talk to she won't go on and on so much. I won't really mind visiting her – at least Lily notices me, I am someone special to her. In the end, Felicity told herself, screwing the lid down on her conscience, it will probably turn out that I am the best thing that has ever happened to Lily!

Lily was still droning on, her voice peevish and flat. Felicity, the sun hot on her back, closed her eyes and counted silently in her head; it was suddenly important to reach three hundred before Lily's voice stopped. Lily finally fell silent at three hundred and three. That must be particularly good, everyone knew that two threes were important. Better still,

Felicity, who had opened her eyes and moved forward around the count of two hundred and fifty, could see that Lily was smiling.

'Oh I *have* enjoyed hearing all about the old days,' she smiled back, 'you must tell me more next time. But I have to go now – I'll tidy up the things first.' Lily made no attempt to detain her as Felicity placed the empty glasses on the tray, hooked the workbag over her arm ('to save you carrying it in later') and made ready to leave. Lily was ready to be left alone, tired but pleasantly so.

When Felicity had finally gone with a last cheery wave before the iron gate swung silently shut behind her, Lily squirmed herself into a more comfortable position in her chair and, eyes closed and face upturned to the sun, dwelt lazily and randomly upon the desultory thoughts that bumbled through her mind like drowsy bees.

It did one good to have someone to talk to now and again, Lily told herself. Maggie Sinclair was all right in her way, but she was not what one could describe as a good listener; not about the past, anyway, always waiting to get her own word in, irritatingly eager to break in with a 'That reminds me of when I – '. The way Maggie went on about her days in the Wrens – just because they'd been allowed to wear underwear of their own choosing they imagined they belonged to some sort of élite! The way she hinted, too, at all the romances she had had – the chances she had let slip by. 'Too many strings to my bow, that was my trouble,' Maggie was fond of saying in a simpering sort of way which was quite ludicrous in a woman of her age. Disgusting, really. More likely she'd made herself too easy to get – otherwise how had she ended up an old maid? When the war had been on, Maggie Sinclair had enjoyed not only the advantage of civilian underwear but had been years younger than Lily. It had required determination to land a husband when one was already in one's thirties and surrounded by so much competition. It had been on the tip of Lily's tongue more than once to point that out to Maggie, but she had restrained herself. After all, it wasn't as though one could afford to turn away friends as one grew more isolated with age.

Felicity was only a child; but such a good listener. Not that she was only a listener: there were days when Felicity talked quite a lot herself. Even Maggie Sinclair listened with interest when Lily passed on the things which Felicity let drop. Well, that was little wonder because they were really interesting little titbits; not the sort of thing one would come by in the normal way of things – not unless one belonged to that sort of circle in the town. Those Winnies with their airs and graces! Who would have guessed that that Joyce Bell had actually stolen a valuable bowl from old Mrs Pewter. Lifted it at a coffee morning and walked out with it under her coat and then, bold as brass, sold it to the antique shop in the High Street! And what about Mrs Pewter's grandchild – Sally, was it? Asked to leave High Beeches on account of her being caught shop-lifting! Of course that lot stuck together, hushed things up – not surprising really, because when one got a glimpse behind the scenes one learned that most of them had something to hide. A case of 'you scratch my back and I'll scratch yours'! It was a pity, Lily mused, that she'd missed that television programme about nudist camps; she'd have liked to have seen it for herself – the sight of Mrs Woodward, naked as the day she came in to the world, playing darts in a pub full of other naked people. Disgusting! Dangerous too, when one came to think about it. Felicity had been at pains to point out that she hadn't watched the programme at home but at Sally Pewter's house as Sally's mother and father had wanted to see what a holiday like that was like as they fancied one themselves. Really!

The heat seemed to be draining away as the sun slid down behind the trees. Lily was not sure whether it was the cooling of the air or the thought of people going about naked that caused her to begin to feel less comfortable. She would soon have to move herself and go inside. Her knees would be bound to give her gyp after hours of inactivity. It was all very well for the doctor to tell her to keep on the move. Take walks, indeed! It took her all her resolution to get the household chores done – and no one could accuse her of neglecting those. Sometimes Lily wished that she could allow herself to ease up on the cleaning and polishing, but she was driven on by a dread of neglected tasks accumulating to a point where it got beyond her and the temptation to 'let things go' might become irresistible.

In the stillness of the garden, Lily turned her head as though she heard something stir. She looked towards the shrubbery where the violet shadows lay long on the grass. Heavy and awkward, she heaved herself out of her chair and stood a moment to regain her breath after the exertion, plucking at her skirt where it clung, clammy with cooling sweat, to her thighs.

She folded up her chair and, letting it drag a little on the ground, carried it slowly back to the cottage. She paused once or twice on the way and glanced behind her as though she thought she was being followed. But the glance was not a nervous one and, when she finally closed the door behind her, it was with a movement no less unhurried than had been her steps.

12

Would individual salt and peppers be too formal? It seemed a pity not to seize the opportunity to show them off. Edith was kneeling in front of the sideboard, a tray nearby on the carpet loaded with the silver which must all be cleaned in readiness for tomorrow's dinner party. Edith would have to get on with cleaning it herself, Mrs Watson had made that abundantly clear. She didn't want to mess up her hands, Mrs Watson had said, silver cleaner had such a roughening effect on the skin and rubber gloves brought her out in a rash. She was anxious to keep her hands in smooth and good condition because she was busy making lots of new clothes for her daughter Gloria. Edith did not believe for one minute that that was true. She was certain that Mrs Watson would outfit her precious Gloria at Marks and Spencer's, with, perhaps, a few special items from Miss Selfridges. No, Mrs Watson had just invented that excuse in order to draw attention, yet again, to Gloria and her achievement. And, of course, there was no denying that it *was* an achievement for the girl to have won a place at Oxford. One should be glad, Edith told herself firmly, that one lived in a society where it was possible for the daughter of one's 'help' to get to Oxford. It just took a little bit of getting used to, that was all.

Mrs Watson was behind her now, puffing and blowing as she leaned across the table polishing its surface with more vigour than might have been exercised if Edith had not also been in the room. One should be thankful that her hands were not also sensitive to beeswax.

'Don't know why you bother with all that silver, myself. Didn't think people went in for that sort of thing nowadays!'

There it was, starting already! With a daughter going to Oxford, Mrs Watson was already setting herself up as an arbiter of taste.

'It just seems a shame to have nice things and not to use them,' Edith murmured, looking sorrowfully at a tiny spoon which had become pitted with salt. 'Besides, it's a good thing to keep up standards – don't you think?'

Miranda never set her table with silver; but Edith was sure that she would if she could. The stainless steel that Miranda went in for was so lifeless and forks with three prongs might be modern but were so inelegant. It was a pity, thought Edith, turning one around in her hand, that one could not give the place-card holders an airing, but with only four guests it would be vulgarly pretentious. They were so pretty, a leaf base supporting a lotus bud fashioned with a slit at the point of the flower where one slotted in the card. At least the holders would be lovely when cleaned, but now they were quite black with disuse and neglect – just as well, perhaps, that there was no need to use them. As it was, there was a frightening amount of work to be got through in a very short time without undertaking any that was not strictly necessary. Fortunately, people did not seem to think nowadays that it was impolite to be given a bare three days' notice of a dinner party. It was Edward who had suggested that Samuel's absence for a whole day and a night should be turned to best advantage. Three days' notice of a funeral was about all one could reasonably expect – death being the ultimate disrupter of the social calendar. It was a happy chance that the funeral was to take place somewhere or other in Buckinghamshire, which circumstance had decided Samuel to spend the night in an hotel.

Samuel rarely missed attending the funerals of his contemporaries and, to that end, brought a ghoulish enthusiasm to his daily study of the Deaths Column. Weddings offered a more conventional opportunity for old friends to get together but, as one became older, their occurrence within one's contemporary circle became something of a rarity.

But, as Samuel pointed out, attendance at a wedding entailed expenditure on a present and a willingness to participate in a great deal of artificial *bonhomie*. A funeral, on the other hand, was a quiet and dignified affair where a gentleman could indulge in sober and sensible conversation and savour to the full the satisfaction of still being around so to do.

While Samuel would be enjoying himself in his own esoteric fashion, Edward and Edith would be dining the new manager of the local building society, whom Edward hoped (in a very discreet way, naturally) to encourage to send a substantial amount of house conveyancing his way. The new manager was, said Edward, an astute and ambitious young man who had already made his name in Round Table circles. The fact that he had a strong, and perhaps to some ears, rather unattractive Midlands accent and that his hair curled over his collar and his shoes (of the laceless type) sported rather high heels, was neither here nor there. All things considered, however, the dinner party was more likely to serve its purpose successfully if Samuel were not present.

But, reflected Edith – in the kitchen now and spreading newspaper over the end of the table preparatory to starting work – one could never predict people's reactions to the impact of exposure to Samuel. There had been a brief phase when Edward, inflamed by injudicious study of the financial press, had nursed feverish and foolish dreams of actually making money as opposed to scraping a living. In furtherance of that uncharacteristic ambition, Edward had thought it politic to cultivate a man who belonged to a strange emergent species of which neither Edward nor Edith had had any previous experience. Edith was still uncertain as to how she should categorise Mr Tyler in her mind. Edward had described him as 'an up-and-coming whizz-kid' and, as Edith was not at all sure what exactly that meant (and Edward's attempted explanation had been very vague), she could only suppose that it was an apt description. When Mr Tyler had been invited to dinner, Samuel, in an access of *folie de grandeur*, had blatantly insulted him throughout the meal. He had even remarked, as piously as though he had been Christ encountering the money-changers in the Temple, that he had never thought to see the day when hucksters and cheapjacks would sit at his board. Mr Tyler had hung on Samuel's every word: the more he had been insulted, the lower he had grovelled. Later, rejecting with ill-concealed contempt Edward's embarrassed attempts to apologise for Samuel's outrageous behaviour, Mr Tyler had sung Samuel's praises and mourned with shaking head the passing of his like. 'One of the last of the old school,' Mr Tyler had said with as much awe in his voice as might be instilled by recollection of an encounter with Attila the Hun. But Edward's bread (not to mention the brandy and liqueurs, thought Edith, still cross at the memory) had been cast upon the waters to no purpose. Mr Tyler had not put any golden opportunities in Edward's way, having reached the conclusion that Edward's humble and bourgeois search for a share of the pickings revealed him as a traitor to his caste and, as such, not to be trusted.

There was no doubt about it, thought Edith, buffing a beautifully balanced serving spoon, the Gordon-Fenn family silver was very beautiful; and where, one might ask, had the money come from for its purchase if not from common trade? Why should she feel that in some way her desire to show it off put her on a par with Samuel? Miranda, she knew, envied her possession of it even if she did pretend that she pitied Edith the work involved in its upkeep. Miranda and Godfrey would complete the dinner party; it was too good an opportunity to miss working off the long outstanding debt of returned hospitality owing. Besides, Miranda was such a talker that it would relieve Edith of the burden of that chore – God only knew what the building society man's wife would be like!

The weather being so warm, a salad and cold cuts would be quite appropriate for the main course and that would give Miranda no opportunity to draw odious comparisons between the quality of her own cooking and that of Edith's. Bottled mayonnaise would never be suspected of its humble origins if served from such a lordly sauce boat, reflected Edith, her tongue nipped between her teeth as she scrubbed at the twiddly bit on the handle with an old toothbrush. Not, of course, that Miranda ever said anything disparaging about Edith's cooking. She didn't need to! But there was something about the inflection with which she pronounced that this or that was 'so unusual' or 'original' that conveyed just what her real opinion was.

Another advantage in serving salad was that it would be inappropriate to accompany such a course with a good wine; lager would not only be correct but, oh joy! so much cheaper. Besides, thought Edith, the young man from the Midlands would surely be more at home with lager.

Mrs Watson had come into the kitchen bringing a disagreeable odour of sweat with her. It was these ghastly synthetic fabrics which she wore, thought Edith, frustrated by the long cuff of her rubber glove in her attempt to reach the handkerchief tucked inside her sleeve.

Mrs Watson put the kettle on for tea. Edith knew it would be tea. Mrs Watson had a theory that to drink coffee in warm weather was a mistake. It heated the blood, she said. She stood watching Edith polishing the filigree fruit bowl and helpfully pointed out with one hand a bit that Edith had overlooked; her other hand remained on the handle of the kettle as though to make it quite clear that her own time was fully occupied with a more important task than the one with which Edith chose to engage herself.

'If you're so set on cleaning up all that old stuff, couldn't you get Felicity to give you a hand with it? My Gloria used to be ever such a help to me in the holidays when she was a kid.'

'I think I would prefer coffee instead of tea,' said Edith, determined not to indulge Mrs Watson's appetite for dragging her daughter's name into every topic. Emboldened by the manner in which she had managed to keep apology out of her voice, she added with nice emphasis, 'if it's not too much trouble for you.'

Mrs Watson shrugged and, with the air of one pandering to a childish whim, managed to drag the coffee-jar towards her without having to move her feet.

'What's she do with her time in the holidays then – your Felicity?'

Edith sometimes asked herself the same question but never with sufficient concern to impel her to seek an answer. There were so many other things which demanded her time and attention. Besides, it was not as though Felicity ever complained of being bored or of not having anything to do. She was a very self-sufficient, quiet child who never gave one cause for worry, and for that I really am truly grateful, Edith acknowledged to herself. Some day soon I really must find time to take her on a little treat – down to the coast for a swim, perhaps. Next week, maybe.

'I don't think Felicity is ever at a loss for something to do. She does all sorts of things – there's her butterfly collection, and she amuses herself in the old tennis pavilion, reading, playing records . . . that kind of thing. You know how it is at that age!'

'Must be a bit lonely for her, though, this summer – what with that friend of hers, Sally, being away in France and you not going anywhere yourselves this year.'

'Felicity could have gone with Sally if she had wanted to. She was invited, you know! But she said that she'd rather stay here, there were other things she wanted to do.' Felicity's rejection of the invitation had struck Edith as a little odd. Spending the summer holidays in a cottage in the Dordogne (even with Sally's mother in charge) seemed a much more attractive proposition than remaining at Westwood. But perhaps Felicity and Sally had fallen out. It could so easily happen at their age when children had a tendency to outgrow old friendships. If they had started to grow apart, it might not be a bad thing, considering that Sally would be going to a different school next term. No knowing what sort of habits Sally would pick up at that beastly Comprehensive – one didn't want Felicity corrupted!

'I did hear,' began Mrs Watson, setting down the cups and showing every sign of settling down to a cosy woman-to-woman chat regardless of Edith's inclinations. 'I did hear as how she's spending quite a lot of time with that Lily Gudgeon.'

Edith, surprised, paused in her struggle to peel off the rubber gloves.

'However did you hear about that?'

'Well, it was when I was in Miss Sinclair's the other day – you know the little sweet shop? Your Felicity was in there at the same time. She was buying a bar of chocolate – funny thing but my Gloria never could eat chocolate! Couldn't as a kiddy and still can't; it brings on a sick headache, you see. The doctor said it was some sort of an allegory. Never had that sort of thing myself, but then Gloria takes more after her father – leastways as far as things to do with the head – "you get your brains from your father and not from your old mum", I tell her, "your dad's the clever half".' Mrs Watson gave a deprecatory little laugh which was wasted on Edith who showed no sign of refuting the statement.

'Now, what was I telling you? . . . Oh, yes. Well, when she went out – your Felicity – Miss Sinclair told me about how she was being ever so attentive to old Mrs Gudgeon. Miss Sinclair would know, her being about the only friend old Lily has! I thought to myself, well there's one for the book, as you might say!'

'How do you mean?' asked Edith, who had succeeded in getting off the remaining glove with a last vicious yank which had scattered a flurry of talcum powder all over the freshly polished silver.

'Well, you know . . . from what I'd heard – not that it's any of my business, like – but old Mr Gordon-Fenn makes no bones about it . . . about there not being any love lost, so to speak, between Lily Gudgeon and Westwood!'

'I suppose you could say that Mr Gordon-Fenn finds Mrs

Gudgeon rather difficult to deal with – unreasonable about some things. I suppose that's true.' Edith, angry at Mrs Watson's intrusiveness, kept her voice cool. 'Mr Gordon-Fenn has been subjected to provocation – but it's really not something I care to discuss.'

'But you did know, did you, about Felicity taking up with her?'

'Taking up! What a curious way you put things, Mrs Watson! Of course I know that Felicity has been visiting Mrs Gudgeon now and again. I think it is such a good sign when the young take an interest in people less fortunate than themselves. I was very pleased when she told me about it.'

That is not exactly a lie, Edith assured herself. Felicity had told her about it, but only after she had tackled her. And as for being pleased – well, what business was it of Mrs Watson how she felt? It had been Kate Pewter who had seen Felicity visiting the cottage and who had thought that she should bring it to Edith's notice. In fact Kate, not content with telling Edith about it, had taken it upon herself to advise Edith that she thought the association ill-advised and that it should be stopped at once. She had even gone so far as to describe the situation as 'dangerous'! Edith would most certainly have adopted the same disapproving attitude herself had not Kate advanced it so bluntly and with such authoritarian heat. Even allowing for the privilege accorded to the elderly, it had surely been little short of impertinent the way in which Kate had berated Edith for not having insisted that Felicity went to France with her grandchild, Sally. Even now the recollection of the conversation made Edith feel very indignant. Could it be that Kate had seen Felicity's rejection of the invitation as some sort of slight to the Pewter family? Even so, she had had no business to accuse Edith of being blind to her child's welfare – what had Kate meant when she had referred to 'the unwholesome atmosphere of Westwood'?

'Yes,' Edith continued, firmly, 'I am delighted that Felicity is doing her best to cheer up the poor old thing. After all, one cannot begin too early to learn that privilege carries responsibility!'

'But does *he* know?'

Edith opened her mouth as though to reply, but then closed it firmly. No, she told herself, this is quite intolerable; there is no reason why I should subject myself to being quizzed by Mrs Watson. I shall be firm and simply refuse to satisfy her impertinent curiosity.

'We really must get on! I want you to give the hall a really thorough cleaning – you can throw out the flowers and leave the bowl by the sink. I'll make a fresh arrangement, although goodness knows when I'm going to find the time.'

To demonstrate that the time for talking was over, Edith began to draw on one of the gloves again. Her skin crept with the cold clammy feel of it. It looked so obscene too, like the flaccid udder of a cow. It had been a mercy, really, Belinda dying. She could never have gone through with all that.

Mrs Watson, seeing the abstracted look on Edith's face, rose with a bad grace, jolting the table so that the silver jangled and rattled.

'You've forgot the cigarette box!' she pointed out, a little mollified at restoring the *status quo*. 'I'll fetch it you,' she added, as though demonstrating her willingness to oblige if not to be ordered.

Edith did not look up when, a few moments later, the silver box was plonked down in front of her with more emphasis than would have seemed necessary.

The merest rub brought up its sparkling sheen. It was an article on which Edith lavished regular care. She handled it lovingly now, just holding it in her hands was a comfort. The inscription she knew by heart and could put faces to many of the engraved signatures on the inside of the lid. Most of them are probably dead by now, she reflected, the young officers who had presented the box to her father 'on the occasion of his marriage, 5th of June, 1928'. Mumsie had left little in the way of a legacy beyond personal effects and of these, this box was the one most treasured by Edith. The furniture Edith had sold. She had felt that her parents' things did not belong in Westwood.

Edward still nursed a grievance against her mother. Only recently, after explaining at tedious length just why a holiday would not be financially possible this year, he had added, 'It was a great pity about your mother.' Edith had realised that the remark was not inconsequent. Nor was Edward expressing grief at the manner of Mumsie's sudden demise the previous year – knocked down by a bus in Bognor.

It had occurred to both of them to wonder how Mumsie managed her affairs so admirably. Despite the slenderness of her army pension and the absence of much capital, Mumsie had somehow managed to contine to live in the house in-herited from her own parents and in a style not noticeably affected by the incursions of inflation. Her life style was generous and hospitable. Every summer the house seemed to be full of old army friends of Mumsie's own generation and, therefore, retired and free to spend a week or two by the sea whenever the fancy took them. Whenever Edward and Edith paid Mumsie a summer visit they invariably found such friends in residence. They would sit about in the garden drinking gin slings and John Collins, basking in the mild sun of the South Coast; the women with leathery, sallow skins and dry, faded hair, the legacy of years lived under brazen and less kind skies. Their talk was of the past : of days in Ismailia, Malta, KL, Aden – the names flung about as though they belonged to parishes in an English diocese. They laughed a lot, like children amused by the craziness of the world in which they now found themselves, a world which was not of their making. Or had they seen themselves as the Olympian adults convulsed by the antics of their infants. Edward had always attributed the levity to the gin.

Edward had come to the conclusion that all these friends of Mumsie paid for their keep. That, he had said, was the obvious answer and the solution to Mumsie's freedom from financial worry. She had turned her home into a discreet private hotel – 'private' only in the sense that it was open exclusively to invited guests. The fear that Westwood might, sooner or later, have to offer shelter to another feckless family pauper was lifted from Edward's mind and he became markedly more genial towards his mother-in-law. He frequently complimented her upon her initiative and financial acumen and Mumsie would modestly concede that she was no fool and smile a secret smile. Edward would smile back, believing the secret to be shared.

It had been a shock for Edward to learn, after Mumsie's sudden death, that the facts had not been as he had supposed.

Mumsie had sold her house to a company in return for a nice fat annuity which had kept her in reasonable comfort and had permitted her to indulge her natural predilection for sharing her good fortune with those whose circumstances were less fortunate than her own. She had indulged her generous impulses to the full and not a penny remained in the kitty. If only she had consulted him, Edward had wailed; just as though it was the lack of Mumsie's confidence that he mourned and not the withering of his financial expectations! Property, particularly on the South Coast, had increased so much in value, there was no denying the fact. Nor could Edward understand why Edith had seemed so little affected by the loss of what might have been a comfortable inheritance. In fact Edith had seemed almost amused that her mother had 'pulled a fast one,' as Samuel so inelegantly and indignantly put it.

On one occasion Mumsie, goaded into retaliation by one of his diatribes against a society which was hell-bent on destroying his rights to privilege, had bluntly told Samuel that it was service families like her own and that of Edith's father which had, over the generations and for paltry financial reward, maintained the peace which had enabled the Gordon-Fenns and their like to make their money. In India, she had elaborated, sizeable fortunes had even been made out of the heavy harvest that death in that disease-ridden land had reaped among the service men and their families. She had glared at the portrait of Samuel's father, who indeed, now that one's attention was drawn to the fact, had the look of an undertaker.

Mumsie had rarely visited Westwood – which had probably been just as well. She had hated Samuel and made little attempt to disguise the fact. She had never referred to him as other than 'Mr Gordon-Fenn' and it was clear that the formality was an expression of her wish for dissociation and owed nothing to respect.

'I do miss you so,' Edith whispered. 'And you!' she added, kissing the letters of her father's name on the silver box. Edith had been in her last year at school in England when her father had died in a swimming accident in Singapore.

Edith sniffed and, her nose full of the acrid smell of metal polish, surrendered herself to the bitter-sweet and insidious comfort of self-pity.

13

'Where exactly is the Third World?' Felicity put the question not so much in a spirit of enquiry, but more in the hope of rousing Lily to some sort of response. While it was encouraging that Lily had, of late, shown an increasing tendency to sink into moods of gloomy introspection, it was no use denying that it was very boring for her visitor.

It was Samuel who had used the term 'Third World' during luncheon. Felicity herself quite liked macaroni cheese, but she could understand why even someone less intolerant than her grandfather might baulk at being presented with it three days running – and in August. It had not escaped his notice, Samuel had said, that a great deal was being written and said about the wisdom of increasing one's intake of pulses, cereals and other 'so-called' natural health foods. Had it not occurred to Edith, he had continued, that the supremacy of Western man, and of the British in particular, had been nourished on a sound diet of good red meat? It was evident to him that Edith, like so many other poor gullible fools, was being influenced by insidious Communist propaganda. Not content with the destruction of the educational system and the relentless undermining of the nation's morals, the Communist infiltrators who controlled the media were now intent upon brainwashing the public into adopting a Third World diet! Before long, Samuel had declared, unless people wakened up to the way in which they were being manipulated, the British nation would be reduced to a race of illiterate, half-caste, apathetic and pot-bellied morons.

But Lily, head bent over her knitting, gave no indication of having heard Felicity's question.

'Isn't it a bit hot for knitting?' Felicity could see that Lily was not actually knitting, but unravelling the work. A bird's nest of crinkly wool was piled on her lap and her lips moved slightly as she kept tally of each undone row. It was the same cardigan which she had been at work upon for weeks, she did not seem to be having much luck with it.

'I spotted a mistake I made earlier. I must get it right: it worries me.'

'Shall I fetch you a glass of squash?' They were sitting under the shade of the copper beech on Lily's little lawn but, even so, it seemed very warm and sticky to Felicity. Just the sight of Lily, so pink and moist, and the hot-looking wool, made her feel itchy.

'Tea would be more refreshing . . . ninety-three. Just make it if you've a mind to.' Lily sounded very irritable.

By the time Felicity returned with the tray, Lily had abandoned her work and lay staring at nothing in particular. She was mindlessly massaging one hand with the other, the slack mottled skin crinkling and sagging disagreeably. Felicity was unpleasantly reminded of a nestful of unfledged birds which she had found in the shrubbery, dead and smelly. Samuel had probably shot the parents.

'Oh dear, I'm afraid the milk's gone off,' she remarked as yellow curds formed on top of the tea.

'Probably.' Lily sounded as listless as she looked. 'This morning I found I had left on the kitchen light and switched off the fridge. Cold chicken swimming in water . . . and the milk was off. Can't think how I came to do anything so silly.' But there was no real sense of puzzlement in her voice. Lily had become used, if not reconciled, to her apparent lapses. But a few sips of the sourish tea seemed to revive her and, switching her gaze from the sun-bleached lawn to Felicity's face, she said –

'I don't know about a Third World. But I do know there is another world. One that one cannot always see, but it's here for all that – around us.'

She really has flipped, thought Felicity, a little uneasy

and glad that they were outside, in full light. Although Lily was looking straight at her, her eyes, between their cushions of fat, were strangely unfocused.

'You think I'm talking nonsense – don't you?'

'No, of course not! But I don't quite understand.'

'Have you never felt the presence of those that have gone before around you? Had a feeling as though they were still there – reaching out?'

Felicity, suddenly but alarmingly aware of more understanding of what Lily was trying to express than she cared to admit, bent forward to scratch at a midge bite on her leg. In that position, her hair flopped over her face and hid it from Lily's view.

'Sort of,' she muttered. She might conceal her face but she could not shut her ears to Lily's voice; Lily talking about things best hidden, best not even acknowledged: the grey shadowy things that lurked somewhere deep down in one's mind, not to be thought about, not to be probed for fear of recognition emboldening them to move forward.

'You know, your grandfather thinks I refuse to get out of this cottage just to spite him. Well, that's part of the truth. But there's more to it than that. You see, I am not as alone here as people might think!'

There was a thin streak of blood now, running down Felicity's leg.

Lily's voice was suddenly sharp, reassuringly worldly. 'You shouldn't scratch like that, you could get blood-poisoning. It can kill you – blood-poisoning! There's some disinfectant in the kitchen, go and dab some on right away.'

The kitchen seemed dark after the brightness of the garden. Felicity was glad that she knew exactly where the bottle was kept, just as she knew where everything else was located in the downstairs rooms. She did not want to linger.

She made herself pause long enough to gulp some water from the tap. She was glad that she had. Her eyes, adjusted now to the change of light, confirmed that Lily's kitchen looked as humdrum as ever. If there was anything . . . well,

H.O.—F

odd . . . in the cottage, she would have been aware of it before this. There was nothing, even in the middle of the night, nothing. That feeling that caught her sometimes at the foot of Lily's stairs, but that was just a draught. Wasn't it? Of course there was nothing here. Not like Westwood. Lily was making something up, probably to account for the odd things that had been happening to her lately. Well, if anyone should know that that has nothing to do with ghosts, I should, Felicity told herself.

She bent down to take another look at her leg. The bite had stopped bleeding; that was good. The sight of blood always made Felicity feel frightened. She kept her head down a little longer remembering Sally's mother's advice when she had nearly fainted the time that Sally had cut her finger on the breadknife.

Felicity was perfectly composed by the time she returned to the garden and Lily took up her story from where she had left off.

Lily was rewinding the unravelled wool on to the ball, pulling it tight to straighten the crinkles. Her voice sounded quite matter-of-fact now, perhaps the mundane task upon which her hands were engaged had something to do with that.

'Of course I don't often see him, only sometimes. But I *feel* his presence a great deal.'

'I've never seen anything here.'

'Well, I don't suppose you would, dear. After all, you are probably nothing to him at all, nothing at all.' Lily sounded a little tart, as though Felicity had shown herself in some way presumptuous. 'But,' she added, more kindly, 'I expect that if he does notice you at all then he regards you with approval – knowing the way you have been such a help in your own little way!'

Felicity was not sure that she liked the sound of that.

'But who is he – I still don't really understand.'

'It's my Jackie, of course – who else? Surely I've told you about Jackie?'

158

So that was Gudgeon's name, 'Jackie', thought Felicity, guiltily aware that she had been in the habit of letting her attention wander when Lily had droned on about her past.

'There is such a thing as love beyond the grave. Which is just as well, considering how hard it is to find it on this side of it!'

'And you think that he comes back here to keep you company?'

'I don't *think*, dear, I *know*! As I said, I don't often actually see him. But sometimes I do, here in the garden. He loved the garden, you see. The garden at Westwood, too, come to that.'

Lily rested her hands and looked round the garden now; Felicity did the same but only out of politeness. The garden looked reassuringly unsepulchral.

'It's upstairs that I see him most often. In my bedroom. That was where he died, you know – in my arms!'

Lily clamped a hand over her mouth to conceal its working. Felicity made herself place her own over Lily's other hand which was clutching and unclutching the mangled knitting on her lap.

'Don't think about it, please!' she murmured. It was the only phrase that came to mind, it was the utterly useless advice which Edith used to urge upon her when Felicity had been going through a phase of nightmares. When I was still a child, thought Felicity.

Lily brought her hand down from her face and grasped Felicity's lean brown fingers in a clammy hold. 'You're a very understanding little person, you know! I've never told anyone else about this before. But lately I've been trying to think about happier days . . . so as not to think about other things which are worrying me just now. Thinking about Jackie's death isn't happy, of course, but remembering him in life and telling someone about him still being here . . . that helps. But it does worry me too – knowing I just couldn't leave him here alone, without me.'

'But if you went to live somewhere else, then he would go with you, wouldn't he?'

'How can I be sure about that? You see, this is the place Jackie knows – where he expects to find me! Oh it's all so difficult. I can't get it straight in my mind.'

'I'm quite sure that he would stay with you wherever you went to live,' said Felicity, very firmly.

'You really think so? Well, he always did have this very good sense of direction – he was never one for getting lost!'

Felicity, with as much caution as she would exercise in pursuing a butterfly preparatory to popping it in her little collector's killing-bottle, said, 'But surely you aren't really thinking about leaving the cottage?'

'Well, I had never intended to. But I have been turning it over in my mind. It might be for the best. None of us gets any younger, you know! But,' she went on with a sudden flare of her old spirit, 'mind you don't breathe a word to your grandfather – I don't want him to have the satisfaction.'

'Grandfather! Goodness, no! *He* doesn't even know that I visit you – Mummy and Daddy know, but Grandfather doesn't. He can be very nasty, you know.'

'Yes, I do know.' Lily's tone was grim. 'Anyway,' she went on as though the very thought of Samuel strengthened her moral fibre, 'nothing's worked out in my mind yet. So don't worry, dear: our little get-togethers are by no means at an end!'

Lily, seeing no joyful relief on Felicity's face (which was hardly surprising as Felicity had been subjected to so many emotions in such a short space of time that her acting talent had become a trifle over-strained), became anxious.

'Perhaps I shouldn't have told you anything about Jackie. You're not afraid now to visit me, are you?'

'No, of course not!' But Felicity was not quite sure what she felt about what Lily had told her – like Lily, she had not yet got things quite straight in her mind.

'There's nothing to be afraid of – really! Jackie doesn't come to frighten, he comes to comfort. It is as though he's a bit of me, like a shadow. That's what people used to say to me, when he was alive, I mean, "Jackie is just like your shadow", they said. He loved me so much. I don't think I was ever shown so much love – before or since!'

Felicity, not feeling able to go through with the hand-patting again, suggested :

'Let me bring you your chocolate peppermints.'

As soon as Felicity had suggested it, she regretted it. Could it occur to Lily to wonder how she knew about the chocolates – hidden as they were in the bureau? Felicity had had a general rummage around the night before when she had slipped in to turn off the refrigerator.

'No, dear. Can't say I fancy anything – what with one thing and another.' Lily, as Felicity had observed, generally derived comfort from a nibble here, a suck there; dulling life's sour edge with a steady ingestion of sweetness. She must be feeling low to refuse the comfort of her chocolates.

'Well, if you're sure that I can't get you anything . . . perhaps you'd like me to go now ?'

Lily did not answer immediately. Her tongue, deprived of anything else to curl around, was roving under her dental plate, rocking her teeth in a very bizarre fashion. Felicity, staring with awed fascination, held her breath until Lily's face resumed its normal contours.

'That's right, dear. You just run along.'

But Felicity did not run. She dawdled across the lawn, careful not to place her feet on the cracks that netted the sun-baked earth. She sneaked one backward glance before she went through the gate. Lily sat, staring ahead, a wisp of gnats above her head but, otherwise, reassuringly quite alone.

The gate closed behind her, Felicity pulled a dandelion head, full-blown, the gossamer tufts trembling. Gently she blew – 'She's leaving, she's not'. The filaments floated away carrying their hard brown seeds on the warm air. 'Lily *must*' – a final puff and the last stubborn seed flew away and a tiny black insect scuttled frantically upon the bare empty button that had been its bed. Felicity threw the stem from her, her fingers sticky with the white milky fluid it had bled. Absent-mindedly, she sucked her thumb and then hastily spat as the rank harsh taste filled her mouth.

Lily sat on, her hands upturned and idle on their woolly nest. She regretted that she had not asked Felicity to help her move her chair from under the shade of the tree before she had left. The air was cooling and a tiny green caterpillar fell from time to time, from the leaves above, upon her heavy limbs, where it arched its bewildered way across the alien surface, observed but undisturbed.

Perhaps I shouldn't have told her about Jackie, thought Lily. I don't really know why I did, unless it was in the hope of reinforcing my belief by sharing it. Years ago when I tried to talk to the Vicar about it, he had shied away, embarrassed. It wasn't as though I had actually told him that I had seen Jackie. I'd just asked him, straight out, if Jackie would be waiting for me . . . somewhere. He'd hummed and hawed and hedged. Some would say this, he had said, others that. If she derived comfort from the belief that she would be with him again, then that in itself, he had said, was a reason for clinging to the belief. Could it be, Lily had pursued in the face of his eagerness to change the subject, could it be that he really was excluded from transition to a life beyond and was tied to the haunts of his life on earth? These, the Vicar had replied, were morbid thoughts, and he had then urged her to join the Ladies' Guild. Talk about asking for bread and being handed a stone! Lily snorted at the memory and, suddenly roused, slapped the creeping caterpillars into a green smear upon her dress.

'None of them are any damned help at all when it comes to the bit!' Lily scrubbed her hand on the underside of her canvas chair, resentment down-turning her mouth. The doctor – what use was he? She'd gone to him a few days before – oh, not about Jackie, that sort of thing not being his province – but to unburden herself of her worries about her increasing forgetfulness, her alarming loss of recall. The things she obviously did, or neglected to do, in moments which thereafter remained blank. The doctor hadn't really listened at all, pulling his prescription pad towards him and writing upon it even as she was talking; just nodding in what was intended to be an understanding way, as though his head were balanced on a wire coil. 'You're just in an anxious phase – nothing to worry about. Not unusual in ladies of your age who live on their own,' he had said. Lily had remembered then that he was also the Gordon-Fenn's doctor and brooded that they might be 'in cahoots'. 'I like living on my own,' she had snapped. 'Of course, of course!' he had replied soothingly, 'very wise, too. You soldier on, Mrs Gudgeon, just soldier on.' The prescription was for a different and, he assured her, slightly stronger, sleeping pill. 'A good night's sleep works wonders – you'll see!' Silly fool, thought Lily; she hadn't said a thing about difficulty in sleeping (as long as she took her pill, she had no difficulty), but he just hadn't listened.

Maggie had listened. But Lily, in retrospect, rather wished that she had not confided in Maggie at all. She had gone to Maggie on the morning that she had come down and found the kitchen under water, the sink tap having been left running and the plug still in the basin. Lily hadn't waited to do more than slosh through the water and turn off the tap. She couldn't face the task of cleaning up – not right away. Lily had grabbed her coat and, fighting against tears, had made her way to Maggie's shop.

Lily must have looked in a state. Maggie had turned the card on the door to 'Closed' and she was not one to turn away business unless she felt there was overwhelming reason to do so. In the little parlour behind the curtain at the back, Lily had poured out her woeful tale. Oh yes, thought Lily as she relived that morning in memory, Maggie had listened all right! She had even poured her a glass of port (although it had scarcely gone ten), but there had been no real comfort to be gleaned from her reactions.

Maggie had been practical in the down-to-earth unsentimental manner which some people could bring to problems which were not their own. She had been so unsurprised; that, thought Lily, was what had been so hard to bear. It was almost as though Maggie had been waiting for this to happen; as though Lily had borne the stigmata of encroaching senility (what else could one call it?) for some time; hidden from herself, but perfectly clear to Maggie – and to how many others?

The wisest course, Maggie had said, looking Lily straight in the eye and barely managing to hide her satisfaction at finding herself in such a dominant position in relation to the independently-minded Lily, would be for Lily to make arrangements to go into some sort of Home. 'There are very nice ones,' she had hurried on, lifting a hand as though to silence Lily's protest. Lily had not been about to protest; not immediately; being far too stunned to say anything. She knew for a fact, Maggie had gone on, that the Home in Southsea where her aunt had spent her declining years had been ideal, and not too expensive. But the great thing was to get *in* while one was still more or less in possession of one's faculties. If you wait until you are really . . . (here Maggie had hesitated as though remembering the need for tact) . . . confused, as it were, then no Home would want to take one on. One could, apparently, go gaga without fear or hindrance once one was actually 'in', because then the Home could find one a bed, without delay, in a suitable State hospital. Maggie had gone on to say, blandly, that it did not matter to one by then where one was, as one would be beyond knowing enough about what was going on to care.

Lily, the warm sweet port increasing the shocked stupor of her brain, had protested as strongly as she was able, which was not much. She had reaffirmed her resolution to live out her days in the cottage. But Maggie had told her that she was only cutting off her nose to spite her face; had urged her to go to Gordon-Fenn (the young one, not the old fellow), and suggest that some offer in the way of an annuity to help pay the Home's charges would ensure her vacating the cottage. 'You could say that the Gordon-Fenns owe you that, when all's said and done,' Maggie had conceded. That, and a great deal more, Lily had thought to herself. At the same time Lily had resolved never to tell Maggie the whole story that lay behind her hatred of Samuel. She was glad, now, that she had stopped herself in the past when she had been on the brink of total revelation. Maggie, she had decided, had proved that she was not a worthy confidante.

Lily had tottered out of the shop, bruised in spirit and encumbered with a bag of assorted sweets which she had felt obliged to buy to recompense Maggie for the time in which customers had been denied access. Maggie, Lily had not been too distressed to notice, had not even knocked off the customary discount she afforded her friend. 'Friend' no more, reflected Lily. It's in times of trouble . . . but she did not even bother to finish the worn phrase in her head.

Lily made a conscious effort to wipe such memories from her mind. Tired as she was, she must summon up energy soon to get out of her chair and move indoors. The sun had almost set, the warmth of the day was seeping away from the garden. The mauve phlox, trembling in the little breeze that had sprung up on the sun's down-going, spilled their heavy sweetness on the air and the sharp beauty of it brought tears to Lily's eyes. 'I thought only onions could do that,' she remarked to herself, dragging the back of a hand across her eyes, which felt strained as well as moist.

Perhaps if we had never come here at all, she reflected, her mind back on a well-worn track, then things might have worked out very differently. If Dad had just held on until the war was over and I had got back home. The three of us could have run the shop very nicely. That future had been in her mind when she had married – no good denying it! The flat waiting there, and all. But I could sense, Lily reminded herself for the hundredth time, I could sense the way the wind was blowing when we came home on leave and I discovered that he'd taken on that Gwen to 'help out'. 'Help out', indeed! Much use that silly piece had been when it came to real work. I told Dad straight, he'd be better off with some lad waiting for his call-up, someone with biceps and a bit of go in him to help hump the heavy stuff around. Bundles of papers and boxes of stock take muscle – I should know, seeing as how it was me that had the heavy side of things all these years. Not that Dad could be blamed for that: lifting Mum had left him with a dicky heart, and no wonder. But he wouldn't listen. Six months and that Gwen had snaffled him. Another three and he'd gone – heart attack. Well, I'd warned him. That Gwen off with a Yank before Dad was cold in the grave. Shop sold, Dad's savings all lining her pockets . . . and off! Don't suppose I'd even have got my hands on the family knick-knacks if it hadn't been for her not wanting to be lumbered with them when she'd join her lover-boy in America. You make your own life, so people say – fine thing if you could!

Lily heaved herself to her feet. The chair would just have to stay out overnight; she was too weary to fold it up.

'Used, that's what I've been,' Lily muttered to the gathering darkness, 'used all my life. Just blown about by the winds of chance.' Heavily she carried herself indoors, her joints stiff, pins and needles prickling in her feet.

In the kitchen, an old cardigan round her shoulders and half a pound of pork sausages spitting companionably in the pan, Lily felt better. Jackie had been there all the time, waiting for her to come inside. She could feel his presence.

'Do you know, Jackie,' she said aloud, inclining her head towards the open sitting-room door because it was there that she sensed he was, sitting in the armchair opposite her own. 'Do you know, Jackie, I wonder sometimes if you are only there because I keep you there. Know what I mean?'

She turned the sausages and added bacon and tomatoes. She didn't expect a reply, even in his lifetime she had never waited for that: just rattling on to him had been a comfort, and still was, although direct reply was now even less anticipated.

'Perhaps there isn't anywhere for you to go on to – nowhere for any of us to go on to, for that matter. I sometimes think that we only live on as long as there is someone left who still thinks about us after we have gone. Now, if I could get that Felicity to really understand about you, then (whatever happens to me) she'd keep you going on – me, too. D'you see? Her just thinking about us, that would do it. Remembering, like.'

Lily dished up her supper and infused a pot of tea. Sitting in front of the fire which had been freshly stirred to life, she ate her meal off the little table and, her mouth otherwise engaged, stopped talking to the empty chair across the hearth-rug from her own. But she glanced at it fondly from time to time.

No, thought Lily, when I really come down to putting my mind to it, I don't really go much on the idea of Heaven. Even less so if the Vicar was of a mind that Jackie mightn't get in. There's a lot of people I wouldn't fancy meeting again, anyway. No, you just die and there's an end to it – and no great loss. But for a little while you sort of go on as long as the ones you left behind still live and think about you. But you go on down here, not in any place up in the sky! A sort of easing off, before the full stop. That's one thing about having kids, they could keep you going for quite a bit. Providing they loved you, that is. Maybe even if they hadn't loved you, but still thought about you and remembered you, now and again.

'You see, Jackie,' she went on, her mouth empty of the last drop of bacon fat and squishy tomato which she had mopped up with a crust of bread, 'my mind fleshes you out. It's my thoughts that make you able to sit there all comfy!'

Lily could see Jackie quite clearly now, his eyes on her. 'At least, I *think* that's how it is,' she added, with less certainty.

14

It was such a relief to be able to yawn hugely, without inhibition, jaws cracking wide, the dry grittiness of one's eyes miraculously soothed and laved with a brief spurt of saline. Felicity rubbed one leg against the other to relieve their prickly discomfort. Her damp knee-socks were gently steaming in the warmth of the fire. Her mother would go on about the grass stains – if she noticed. Why don't you just go bare-legged, Edith sometimes suggested. Brambles and nettles, that was why. Jeans were the answer. Everybody had jeans. Mummy said that that was a very good reason for *not* wearing them: they were hobbledehoy, unfeminine – and, besides, Grandfather would be bound to create.

Lily was taking a long time, just making a pot of tea. In one sense that was a relief but, in another, it was irritating. Felicity couldn't get away now until they had drunk it.

It had all got so boring. The holidays were practically over and they'd been wasted. The summer was almost over, too, and it had all trickled away like water in her hands. It would be too awful if she had just wasted her time! Sally would be back from France next week, full of chat and 'oh, you *should* have been there'. Lily had been going batty anyway, hadn't really needed all that effort to push her nearer the edge of decision. All that Felicity had achieved had been to make Lily face the alternative of a Home and that consideration had only hardened her resolution not to leave the cottage. Lily kept going on and on about 'not giving that Maggie the satisfaction' and that she couldn't bear the thought of nurses in a Home ordering her about and telling her what to do! Felicity glared at the bowl of drooping dahlias on their doily in the middle of the table; the water in her eyes made them shimmer like obscene hunks of raw wet liver.

Lily thumped into the room with the tea tray. Her feet were encased in huge home-made slippers made, as she had proudly explained to Felicity, out of scraps of wool worked with a rughook on sacking. Her feet looked like multi-coloured hedgehogs. The sudden change to rain had made Lily's feet swell, or so she maintained; unfortunately the dry warm weather had had much the same effect; the cold brought on her rheumatism 'something cruel' and wind activated her lumbago. Felicity scowled at Lily's back with loathing.

Lily blew on her tea, but with a certain genteel discretion. It was the tremulous quiver in the hairs that sprang from the mole at the side of her mouth that betrayed her. Felicity got up and fetched the milk-jug from the tray. She wanted to scream.

'Thank you, dear,' Lily remarked as she handed back the jug. 'You look tired – a bit washed out, as though you need a good sleep.'

'I'm OK. I get lots of sleep, thanks.' Well, that wasn't quite true, but at least she had been getting more than a normal quota of rest. Felicity had remained in her bed through the hours of darkness for several nights now. It wasn't that she really believed in Jackie's presence in the cottage, or so she told herself, but her nocturnal activities in the cottage had begun to seem pointless. Besides, lethargy had blocked her inventiveness.

'School starts next week.' Felicity offered the information in a vague effort to explain her obvious flatness. As soon as I've drunk this – I'm off! she told herself. It had stopped raining, but the room was still dark, the greenery outside, dark with summer's dying, seemed to crowd round the little windows, greedily devouring air and light.

Lily bent down and placed her still half-full cup on the tiled hearth. Felicity could hear her corset creak slightly as she straightened and her movement released a faint whiff of scented talcum on the air. Her hands now free, Lily polished her glasses on the hem of her skirt and settled them carefully again on her face as though she were determined to see quite clearly the effect on Felicity of what she was about to say.

'I have never told you how my Jackie died.'

It was not so much a statement of an omission as a preamble to its rectification. Felicity recognised the tone, she had heard it often enough in her grandfather's voice. She had been moving herself to the edge of her chair as a preliminary to taking her leave, but now wriggled a few inches back and tried not to glower as Lily's eyes were on her.

'Your grandfather murdered him.'

Felicity, already embarked on the process of settling her face into an expression of polite attentiveness and disengaging her mind from the immediate, took a couple of seconds to register what Lily had said. The words, when they did impinge, had the unnerving quality of an echo.

Lily's face, as she observed the shock register on Felicity's, looked as smugly satisfied as it did when she bit into a chocolate and found the filling to be her favourite strawberry cream.

'He . . . he couldn't have!' Felicity's voice was thin, unreal.

'And I'm telling you that he did. Seeing as how I *saw* it, I should know!'

'But Grandfather's never been in prison . . . or anything. You go to prison if you kill someone!'

'I'm telling you what happened. I'm not saying justice was done, am I? Retribution, well that's a horse of a different colour.'

'Nobody's ever said . . .'

'Well, they wouldn't, would they? Besides, it happened long before you were born, back in '64. I wouldn't be surprised if your mother doesn't know about it – I expect there's quite a lot she doesn't know about the Gordon-Fenns. But your father knows all right! And your grandmother, she knew all about it. Samuel's poor wife knew a lot that she never let on about – or, if she didn't, then she was a greater fool than she appeared to be.'

'My grandmother wasn't a fool! She was beautiful and knew all about how to make everything fun, and everything. . . .' Felicity's voice tailed off.

'Well, you never knew her, did you, dear? But she couldn't have been very clever to have married a man like your grandfather, now could she? Not that I had anything against her. More sinned against than sinning, you might say.'

'How could Grandfather have . . . how could he do that and not get found out?' There was challenge in Felicity's voice.

'He shot Jackie. And he was found out. There was no question but that he did it. But it was called an accident. An accident!'

Perhaps it was true. That did sound like Grandfather. Shooting things the way he did. But it could have been an accident then.

'It wasn't an accident. I can tell you that for sure!' Lily sounded as though she had guessed what was passing through Felicity's mind.

'It's as fresh in my mind as though it happened yesterday. Jackie was out in the garden, you see – your garden, as it happened. I was going to fry him a bit of liver and bacon for his tea. Do you know, liver and bacon was almost his favourite thing! Well, you know how it is with liver – you mustn't cook it too long, else it goes leathery. So I wanted him ready and waiting, as it were. I called him, but I couldn't see any sign of him, so I guessed he was up at the far end of the garden. I was right. Jackie was up there, this side of the tennis court, where the shrubbery is.'

Lily paused, a hand working at the clumsy pebble brooch at the neck of her dress.

'Get me another cup of tea, dear. Just calling it to mind makes me . . .'

'No,' Lily said, so abruptly that Felicity nearly lost her

balance, bending as she was to retrieve Lily's cup from the hearth.

'Get me a brandy – there's a little bottle in the sideboard. For emergencies.'

Felicity found the bottle, a glass; poured from one into the other. She watched her hands accomplish these things as though they acted independently of her mind.

Lily downed the brandy as though it had been a draught of medicine.

She sat silent, staring into the glass as though puzzled to see it empty.

'He was up near the shrubbery?' Felicity prompted, wanting it over with.

'I wasn't more than a few feet away when it happened. He, your grandfather, must have seen me. But it didn't stop him, not him! He wanted me to see that it was deliberate. Not that I saw him, not right away. Well, it all happened so quick. My eyes were on Jackie. Then, all of a sudden, there was this shot and Jackie was on the ground – right there, almost at my feet. There was this awful scream. That was me. It was funny that: looking back, I could hear the scream as though it didn't come from inside me at all.' Lily paused, staring at Felicity, but her eyes seemed to be looking through and beyond her.

'I got down beside him and I still wasn't thinking about the shot – I was only thinking about Jackie. But I must have looked up through the bushes, looking for someone to help me. Sort of instinctive. From down there I saw him – Samuel, skulking in the pavilion. He was leaning on the rail at the front by the end pillar as though he'd been steadying himself for the shot. You could see it hadn't been an accident – well, it's hard to explain, but you could just tell he'd been waiting there, deliberate like, for Jackie to come into view. I shouted something; I couldn't tell you for the life of me what it was. But I'll never forget what he yelled back! "Bugger you" – that's what it was. And then he was off, back into the pavilion. Like as not he was drunk.'

'Was Jackie dead – right off?'

Lily shook her head. 'I got him back to the house. My legs like jelly.' Lily pressed a hand over her mouth. It seemed as though a few minutes went by before she continued. Petals dropped from an overblown dahlia on to the table, the susurration seeming loud in the quiet of the room.

'He died up there, on my bed. I just knelt there, my head down level with his. I was afraid to leave, to go downstairs to telephone. Well, I could tell he was finished. It was his chest, you see: must have got the lung. Not a sound did he make, blood coming out of his mouth and his eyes on me. On me, until they went dull.'

'But the police!' Felicity's voice almost pleaded. After all, she thought, clutching at any straw to enable her to dismiss this nightmare as a fantastic taradiddle, even Grandfather couldn't go about shooting people dead and not be called to answer for it.

Lily, suddenly matter-of-fact and scornful, clapped her hands angrily on the arms of her chair.

'I told you – didn't I? *He* said it was an accident – said he was after rats. Had his eye on one in the bushes, he said, fired when he saw it moving and that was how he got Jackie. Didn't know Jackie was there at all – that was what he said. Well Jackie stood higher than a rat – even your grandfather couldn't deny that. But he had an answer to that, too. Said it was suddenly seeing me coming up to the edge of the shrubbery that startled him just as he was pulling the trigger. That made the gun jump, so the shot went high. Trying to make it look as though it was somehow my fault – can you imagine!'

'But if you were so sure . . . I mean, how did the police just take Grandfather's word – just like that?'

'You might well ask! Well him and the Commissioner were thick as thieves. Your grandfather played golf in those days. That and used to have some high-up policemen to dinner. It was all wheels within wheels. Anyway, that's what they came up with at the end of the day – accident! And not content with what he did, your grandfather hounds me to get out of this cottage. Takes my husband, my Jackie, and now wants to rob me of the roof that's over my head. That's Samuel Gordon-Fenn, Esquire.'

15

Surely that was Felicity? Kate Pewter screwed up her eyes and peered into the middle distance. The pavement, grey and faintly glistening with recent rain, stretched like a strip of silk ribbon to the brow of the cul-de-sac, empty save for the one figure. Felicity was not exactly dawdling, but there was no spring in her walk. Some type of bag bumped against her legs. She must be on a shopping errand again for that Gudgeon woman – otherwise she would have returned home by the garden. Kate made an impatient tck with her tongue. Edith had obviously paid no attention to what she had said all these weeks ago when she had first realised that Felicity had struck up some sort of relationship with the Gudgeon woman.

Kate stood irresolute. She had been about to cross the road to her own house which stood on the corner of the avenue (once the drive to her old home) which now served the trim little houses which Samuel scornfully dismissed as 'rabbit hutches'. Kate, her letters written and a few minutes earlier posted in the box, knew exactly what it was that she wanted to do. She would make herself a nice long drink – lemon, she thought, with just a touch of brandy and ice – and listen to a programme on the radio. Friends were coming round for a rubber of bridge in the evening and she wanted a little quiet time before getting ready for their arrival. But . . . irritated by her own concern, still she hesitated on the edge of the pavement. There was something faintly disturbing about that lone figure. She couldn't put a finger on it, but something was wrong.

Chiding herself for her inability to do otherwise, Kate began to walk towards Felicity. She walked slowly. The sun skulked somewhere behind the rain clouds and the damp air that rose from the wet road and clung to the dripping trees robbed the atmosphere of all vitality. Well, thought Kate, it was, after all, the tag end of summer: always a spent, tired season. It would be September in a couple of days or so and the thought of approaching autumn lifted Kate's spirits. All that riotous colour, that celebration of fecundity come to jubilant fruition! Kate could never understand why many people dreaded autumn and regarded it as the death of the year. It was now, when the eyelid of nature drooped, weary, that she found the testing time. Perhaps, she told herself, that was all that ailed Felicity. The child was herself at the age when one teetered on a brink between two seasons; a vulnerable stage, sharp with unsought, intuitive understanding and clouded with emotional confusion.

Felicity, her eyes on the pavement, did not look up even when the slap, slap of Kate's old *espadrilles* on the flags must have been quite audible.

'Hullo, Felicity!' Kate had planted herself straight in Felicity's path. If Kate's appearance had startled her, Felicity's face did not betray it.

'Doing some shopping for Lily Gudgeon, are you?' Kate went on, determined to reach behind that impassive look.

Felicity shook her head. Kate's eyes had dropped to the shopping-bag — what a monstrosity, she thought: raffia, embroidered with large daisies in puce and acid yellow, loose strands hanging from it in tufts like the pelt of a mangy animal. But Felicity's eyes did not follow Kate's gaze; she held the bag as though she were unaware that she carried it.

Kate slipped a hand round Felicity's arm, feeling, under her light grasp, the slender bone construction with faint distaste. I will not, she told herself, permit myself to be reminded of Edwina.

'Do you know,' she confided, making her voice chirpy and glad that Felicity was too preoccupied to detect the contrived cheerfulness, 'I was just thinking how nice it would be to have a bit of company — and then I spotted you coming along the road! Wasn't that a bit of luck?'

Felicity murmured something which Kate had no option but to regard as an attempt at polite interchange. She rattled on: how depressing the weather was, how Felicity must be quite relieved that school would soon be starting again. Inconsequential nothings which merited no serious reply and, receiving none, no offence needed to be taken.

Felicity was piloted across the road, up Kate's trim little path and was seated in a plump chintzed chair without any show of resistance. It was only when Kate asked her whether she would prefer a fruit drink or a 'fizzy' that Felicity seemed to drag her mind into focus.

'I mustn't wait, really – I ought to be getting home.'

But Kate gave her a little push back on to the cushion behind her. 'Nonsense, my dear. Surely there's no hurry? I'll just go and fix us something long and cool – I'm so parched!'

When she returned to the room, Kate found Felicity sitting on the edge of her chair. She was shaking, her arms were crossed, fingers clutching her shoulders. It would have been less disturbing if she had been crying.

'Tell me!' Kate spoke firmly, quietly standing in front of Felicity; not touching her, but holding out the glass of fruit juice with an authority that demanded that Felicity should reach out and take it.

'Mrs Gudgeon . . .' Felicity stopped. Both her hands were now tightly round the glass and her hands, in their turn, gripped between her knees as though to prevent the liquid being spilt by their shaking.

'Mrs Gudgeon . . .' she began again, not looking at Kate. 'She told me about Grandfather and her husband.'

Kate stepped back and was glad to feel the edge of the sofa, firm and stable, behind her knees. She sat down abruptly, not taking her eyes off Felicity's face.

'About . . . about how Grandfather murdered him!'

'He *what?*' The tension had drained out of Kate's body and the words burst out explosively.

'Oh I know it was covered up . . . that they pretended it

had been an accident. But it wasn't, was it? He really did it –
shot him! That's what he did. Grandfather is a murderer, a
real murderer!' Felicity's voice had risen to an hysterical
pitch.

'Stop it at once, Felicity! *Stop*. Do you hear me?' Felicity,
reacting to the harshness of Kate's tone, began to cry.

'There now. That's better!' Although God knows if it is,
thought Kate, wishing herself far away. It's like finding oneself suddenly in the middle of a mine-field. Why the hell,
God, did you place this wretched child in my path at this
precise moment? Well, I expect You know what You are
up to, Kate added, hastily, in her mind. After all, if she
expected Him to guide her feet out of this one, then it was
wiser to adopt a respectful tone.

'I don't know what nonsense Lily's been filling your head
with – but I can assure you that your grandfather never
killed anyone in his life!' Well, not by actually shooting
them dead, Kate amended in her mind.

'But she *told* me . . .'

'Now, let's just start there. Just what *did* she tell you?'

'About Grandfather shooting Jackie in the garden and him
dying on her bed and now he sorts of haunts the cottage
and . . .'

Kate silenced the jumble of words with a sudden clap of her
hands.

'*Jackie*, you said?'

Felicity nodded, impatient to rush on.

'Well, for a start, that wasn't Gudgeon's name! Can't
recall off-hand what it was. He was always referred to as
just "Gudgeon" – you know how it is. But I did know it
once, and it certainly wasn't Jackie!'

Kate suddenly snapped her fingers.

'But of course! Jackie was the name of her beastly dog.
That was it, Jackie! A sort of a Jack Russell thing crossed
with something else equally disagreeable.'

Felicity was staring at her. She was trying to remember
just how she had assumed that Jackie had been Lily's husband.

178

She shook her head as though to disentangle the threads that snarled her thoughts.

'You're just trying to put me off. Lily said it was,' she struggled for a second to find the phrase. ' "all wheels within wheels",' she finished.

'Don't be ridiculous, child! You've just got it all wrong – and I don't blame you entirely. God knows, that woman thought more of her dog than she ever did of poor Gudgeon. It's little wonder that you got the wrong end of the stick. Now, you just listen to me.'

Felicity made no move to interrupt, so Kate paused to take a drink from her glass. She had been clutching it so tightly that it felt quite warm on her tongue. Never mind, she consoled herself, it's wet and has just enough brandy to keep my mind sharp.

'That's better!' She smiled at Felicity and put the glass, half-empty now, on the table at her side.

'Your grandfather – far from doing him the least harm – was very fond of Gudgeon. Or perhaps I should say that he valued him both as a good gardener and for the type of person he was.' Kate paused, her eyes downcast, the thumbnail of her right hand working at the cuticules on the nails of her left. Words, nuances, she thought – or need I be so careful? A child of Felicity's age . . . but then nowadays, what with television and so forth, one never knows what they understand or don't understand. God help me! But the phrase sprang to her mind not as an invocation but as a wry comment on her own uninvited predicament.

'You probably know that your grandfather brought the Gudgeons here after the war. Gudgeon had been his clerk in the army – or something of that sort. Well. Lily was far from a loving wife to the poor man. At least, that was the impression one got. Perhaps she just hadn't approved of him becoming a gardener. I don't know. Anyway, take it from me that she was beastly to him. But she had this wretched animal, Jackie, and he got all her affection – perhaps if they had had children it would have been different.'

179

Felicity, her eyes not leaving Kate's face, had leaned back in her chair and was sipping her drink. Still wary, but at least attentive, as Kate observed with satisfaction. Kate, confident now, her hands still and her eyes calmly fixed on the girl, continued with the story.

'That dog – "*my* Jackie" as Lily always called the wretched yapper – hung round her all the time. He sort of ganged up with her against Gudgeon. It's hard to describe, but there was something weird, unwholesome, about it. I saw it for myself. The dog would snarl at Gudgeon. Jealous, perhaps, I don't know. But I am sure Lily egged him on. He used to snap at Gudgeon too, nip at his ankles – that sort of thing. One got the feeling that that dog longed to physically attack Gudgeon in a way his mistress secretly longed to do. He was a kind of extension of Lily.' Kate stopped herself, a little dismayed at her own fanciful thoughts. Felicity needs down-to-earth talk, not imaginative ramblings. She had obviously heard enough of those already!

'Well, one day Jackie did bite Gudgeon really badly. A nasty, deep bite – somewhere about the calf of his leg. Gudgeon apparently didn't pay much attention to it at the time and Lily made even less of it – just stuck a plaster on the wound to stop the bleeding, something like that. Anyway, the following day the leg was quite stiff and painful and Gudgeon sent word to Samuel that he wouldn't be able to get on with any gardening for a day or two.

'Samuel went down to the cottage to see him and when he saw the state of the leg he was very concerned. He phoned for the doctor but, or so it turned out afterwards, by the time the doctor arrived, poor Gudgeon was feverish and a bit delirious so it was Lily who did all the talking. The doctor said (this was at the inquest, you see) that at no time was he told anything about a bite because Lily just gave him a history of Gudgeon having been taken ill, temperature, headache, that sort of thing. The doctor just gave him the usual routine sort of examination – never thought of pulling down the bedclothes and looking at the man's legs (well, one wouldn't, would one?). There was a lot of 'flu going the rounds at the time and the doctor thought that Gudgeon just had a bad bout of that. He left a prescription and told Lily to get in touch if things didn't improve.

'Samuel called after the doctor's visit but Lily wouldn't let him see Gudgeon – said he was sleeping. Perhaps he was, I don't know. She never had liked Samuel, you see.

'By the time your grandfather did manage to see Gudgeon a couple of days later – forced his way in, or so he said – the poor man was almost beyond help. Samuel got him taken to hospital. But he died soon after – extensive blood-poisoning.'

Kate paused to finish her drink. She had Felicity's rapt attention now.

'On the day of the funeral your grandfather was pretty upset. Well, really *very* upset – and angry. I think that perhaps he got a little drunk when he got back from the cemetery. In the afternoon he went out into the garden with his gun.

'Jackie did get shot. That is quite true. Lily made more fuss about the death of that dog than she did about poor Gudgeon's death – there's no two ways about that! Called the police, made a great song and dance. Threatened to sue. The woman seemed quite unhinged.

'Now that, Felicity, is the truth of it.'

Or as much as you need ever know about Samuel and Gudgeon, thought Kate, smoothing her frock over her knees and feeling that she had done rather well.

'A dog!' Felicity gave an embarrassed little laugh and suddenly stretched her body, kicking out her legs which had been tightly tucked close into her chair. Her sudden movement overturned the raffia bag which lay nearby.

'Whatever have you got in that extraordinary bag?' Kate asked, eager to divert Felicity from what had gone before.

Felicity looked down at the bag and appeared almost puzzled to see it there.

'Oh that! I don't know, yet. Lily handed it to me, just as

I was leaving, I think. She said something about it being a present to help me keep her in mind, her and Jackie, something peculiar like that!'

'Do let's have a look – go on, surprise me!'

Felicity reached into the bag and pulled out a package which was wrapped in layers and layers of tissue paper. The tissue had originally come from the baker's wrapped round bread. Lily was a great one for hoarding paper-bags, string and plastic containers.

As Felicity unwound the paper, hard little breadcrumbs, like grains of sand, were sprinkled on the carpet. Kate watched them fall with happy unconcern – in the last few minutes the Aubusson had come so perilously near to having had something much more ineradicable spilled upon it!

'Oh!' Felicity gave a little gasp of delight as she unrolled the last sheet of paper.

'See – it's one of the little cottages. What a darling!' She cupped her hands round the object and gazed at it in silence.

Kate, curious to discover what could have produced such an attitude of rapt adoration, rose and stood at Felicity's side.

'Isn't it just . . . the dreamiest . . . just *beautiful*.' Felicity had slipped the porcelain piece on to her lap and was running a thin finger delicately over the little pointed gables, the chimney-pot and the orange-coloured front door.

'See!' she said, insinuating the point of a nail between the latticed bars of the casements, 'it's hollow inside!'

She turned it over on her lap, as gently as though it were an eggshell. Having seen only the front of the cottages through the glass doors of Lily's cabinet, it came to Felicity as a disappointing surprise to see the back revealed.

'The back's nothing but a big hole – look, you can get your fingers in. There's nothing inside, it's just *empty*!' The distress in her voice seemed out of proportion.

'Wait. May I?' Kate leaned over and lifted the piece from Felicity's lap and placed it on the little side table.

'These little things were made to hold a small candle,

usually one made with perfumed wax. That's why the back is quite plain with a hole – just like this one – big enough to get the candle in place, you see. This really is a very nice example – fancy Lily Gudgeon having something like this!'

And fancy Lily giving it away, thought Kate, wondering once more exactly what Felicity and Lily saw in one another.

'She's got several. They belonged to her mother. But I thought it would be . . . well, real all over. Real inside too. You know . . . ?'

'But you see,' Kate tried to explain, 'one places it so that one only sees the lovely front. Once the candle is inside and alight, it looks even more enchanting. But one must use a good beeswax candle, not something inferior that would smoke and smell nasty. Look at the lovely little flowers round the door.' Privately, Kate thought they were crude and vulgar, but she was making an effort to rekindle Felicity's enthusiasm which had so sadly evaporated.

Felicity leaned forward to look more closely at the flowers and exclaimed, 'Look – there's a fox there, by the bush at the front door!'

'My word, so there is!' Kate peered at the lean tan shape skulking below a tiny viridian knob of green, which looked more like a cabbage than a bush.

'I expect it shows up much better when the light shines through the windows.' The predator that lurks at the door, Kate thought, oddly disturbed.

'You see, just like a real house, this one really needs a light within. Do you understand, Felicity?' The question was tentative, Kate's tone a little embarrassed.

But Felicity gave no indication of having heard. She seemed to have become partly reconciled to the cottage's short-comings and was again fingering its glaze.

What am I trying to do? thought Kate. People never do hear anything until they are ready for it; and then it's generally too late.

Felicity was wrapping the paper round the cottage again. 'Fancy,' she said, 'I never noticed the fox before!'

The rain had started again by the time Felicity took her leave. Kate insisted that she borrow the old umbrella that had belonged to her husband. She stood at the door and watched her go, the long coltish legs in their grubby white socks scissoring below the black toadstool spread of the umbrella. Her gait was still odd, but this time, as Kate observed, it was because Felicity was carefully avoiding treading on the pavement cracks.

Kate closed the door, a little reassured. Felicity was, after all, perhaps not so different from any other child.

16

Felicity, wide awake, snapped on the bedside lamp. Grandmother Edwina's travelling-clock in its shagreen case showed her that it was ten to four. Beside the clock stood the china cottage, the light from the low standing lamp shone through it, illuminating its emptiness.

What was it that Lily had said? Something about a little gift which would help Felicity to keep her in mind; never to forget her. It seemed to work. Lily was not just 'in' Felicity's mind but very much on it.

Felicity lay back on her pillow. She jerked the blanket over her shoulder and lay on her side, staring at the cottage. Lily and her blood-curdling story – and it was only about a dog! She'd even produced a bedspread from the bottom drawer of her bureau to show Felicity the bloodstains which she had never rinsed out. My memento something-or-other, she had called it. She had kissed the largest stain, her lips rasping on the crusted linen thread. Felicity moved her legs restlessly, embarrassed by the memory of her own horror – and all over a dog! No wonder she had only the haziest impression of the other things Lily had subsequently said – babbling on. There had been a great deal about her not being able to bear the thought of people being in control of her, telling her what to do, ordering her about.

But it had been unusual, the way Lily had escorted her to the front door instead of letting her run home through the back garden. It was not as though she had asked Felicity to get something from the shops. There had been something formal in the way she had opened the door for her. Was it that Lily did not expect Felicity to visit her again? Could it be that Lily had at last made up her mind to go away? For all her protestations that she would *never* leave the cottage and enter a Home, she still might one day – one had to cling on to that hope.

Was Lily perhaps going away for a little holiday? Felicity flung herself on her back. If only she could remember more of what had been said – but her mind had numbed; or stuck like a gramophone needle on Lily's story and that ghastly bedspread. Lily did have cousins, somewhere: Ellie and Glad. Had she mentioned them again that afternoon? Said something like, 'I'm going to Ellie and Glad's for a little holiday'?

Why did I go and blab it all to Mrs Pewter? Felicity asked herself, thumping the mattress with her fists at the memory. She must have thought I was an idiot – thinking it was Gudgeon that Lily had been talking about! But if I hadn't told her, then I would still think Grandfather had murdered old Lily's wretched husband. I bet Mummy doesn't know about Jackie – Daddy might. Well, it doesn't really matter now.

I'll move that china cottage later, Felicity promised herself. It could be that it's that that fills my mind with Lily. After all, Edwina's things make her seem to come really close, just as though she had never died at all. If I hadn't hidden her beads and things down in the pavilion, I could hold some of them now, and then she would be here – not bloody Lily. Bloody old Lily, bloody old Lily and her beastly dog, Felicity muttered in an attempt at exorcism.

Felicity switched off the light and lay still in the dark, her eyes on a thin wand of pale light that lay across the ceiling. There was moonlight outside: piercing through the crack where the curtains did not quite meet.

I could, she thought, go down to the pavilion now and bring back some of Edwina's things. I suppose I could keep them hidden here somewhere. I wouldn't want Mummy to find them. She'd ask questions about where I had found them and then, perhaps, go poking about in that trunk in the attic and send all those lovely clothes to a beastly jumble.

Or, worse still, she'd cut them up to make something else! She had made a terrible party cloak out of an old crimson dressing-gown that had belonged to Dora. Felicity shuddered at the memory. I'm going to get some of Edwina's things, right now, she told herself, suddenly making up her mind.

Felicity slipped out of bed, turned on the overhead light; at least that did not spotlight the cottage the way the other did. Over her pyjamas she put on her dark school gaberdine coat with the hood which hid her pale hair, thrust her feet into her plimsolls, and she was ready. The small torch was already in her coat pocket, this being Felicity's prowling uniform.

The house was silent. Puss-puss slept peacefully in his basket in a corner of the kitchen, he opened his eyes when Felicity crept in, stretched his legs and with a little chirrup that was scarcely a miaow, relaxed and slipped back into sleep. Felicity took some biscuits from their tin. The night was quite warm, she could sit in the pavilion for a little while and see if any moths came to the battery lantern which she kept there.

Beetles scuttled on the floor of the laundry, black and shiny in the beam of her torch. Underwear, snatched from the garden line from the day's rain, gleamed faintly in the gloom from the rope slung across the room. Felicity ducked, but one of Samuel's long cotton vests slid wetly across her cheeks.

Outside, the garden was bathed in chill, silvered moonlight. The last of the day's rain-clouds, driven by a brisk westerly breeze, scurried across the face of the moon and, to the left, the sky glowed sickly yellow from the lamps of the motor-way that ran, unseen, at the foot of the slope.

The path that Felicity took to the pavilion was, through frequent use, well-trodden, like a rabbit run. She had almost reached the pavilion when the fancy took her to turn aside from the path and take a look at the old cherry tree. It frequently wept glutinous resin and sap from the wounds inflicted by the rubbing of its neglected limbs one against the other. Moths, as Felicity knew, were attracted to the viscous discharge. She waded through the cow parsley, its leaves rubbing rough against her hands and the flowers, bruised by her passage, tainting the air with a musty smell.

Felicity moved stealthily as she approached the tree but, despite her care, a flurry of tiny moths took to the air; but one remained. Drained of its colour in the moonlight, it was still instantly recognisable. Felicity caught her breath with excitement at the sight of the large moth which clung to the bark of the tree. Its wings trembled slightly as it sucked the sap. But no one could mistake the significance of the skull-like device etched on the back of its velvety head.

Felicity had long coveted a death's-head hawk moth to add to her collection. If she turned back now to get her net and killing bottle from the pavilion, she might find the moth gone on her return. Gently, holding her breath, she stretched out her hand and, between finger and thumb imprisoned its fat body. As she plucked it from the bark, it squeaked. Startled, she released her hold and watched it flutter from her.

Angry with herself, she banged her hand against the tree. She should have remembered! She had read that the death's-head could make a noise: something to do with the air being forced down its tongue when frightened. She could have wept with vexation. I'll never have a death's-head now – not ever, she told herself, kicking the tree for good measure. A bird flew from the branches above, breaking the silence of the night with a clatter of wings.

Felicity leaned her head against the tree trunk. Nothing had gone right, all day long, nothing. She couldn't even feel pleased about getting her hands on one of Lily's cottages at last. Even that hadn't quite come up to expectations. Damn Lily. Damn, damn, damn. The holidays nearly over and still the horrible woman crouched in that cottage like a great toad despite all Felicity's scheming and contriving.

But Lily *must* go, Felicity told herself, rubbing the toe of one foot against the calf of the other leg to ease the dull pain where she had rashly kicked it against the tree. For all that she had said about not leaving, there was no doubt Lily was at least *thinking* about it. One last try might do it. But what? Perhaps if she went back to the cottage, just once more, something would occur to her. Switch on the electric kettle with no water in it, perhaps? That seemed a bit tame. Pinch some things from the house and leave a window open so that Lily would think she had had a visit from a burglar? That sounded better. There must be *something*. Just one more try.

Felicity slipped her hand in her pocket, yes, as she had suspected, the key to the cottage was still there. She had forgotten to replace it on the board in the laundry-room the last time she had made a night visit. The decision to *do* something lifted her spirits. Besides, she thought, she wanted her own back on Lily for having so frightened her that afternoon. Felicity knew, too, now, that a ghostly Gudgeon did not haunt the cottage. Jackie was only a dog. Animals didn't have spirits that could haunt like humans – or did they? Anyway, it was all just taradiddle!

Full of purpose, Felicity skipped through the garden, hands in pockets, one grasping the heavy iron key, the other round the torch which was not needed to light her way along the moon-washed path.

Lily's kitchen smelt soapy. For some reason everything seemed more obsessively clean than ever. On the table in the sitting-room a little pile of envelopes lay, unstamped but with some silver by them. The coins held down a scrap of paper which read 'Please post'. Perhaps Lily had meant to leave the letters and the money at the back door for the milkman. The milk account book was also on the table with a £1 note and thirty pence on top of it. Lily, thought Felicity with satisfaction, really was getting very absent-minded – and all on her own, without any help from Felicity!

She stood for a moment, gently drumming her fingers on the table-top, wondering what she could do. Everything was so tidy; except the hearth, she suddenly noticed. Lily must have been burning old papers or letters, little bits of charred paper had drifted on to the normally pristine tiles. The brasses looked even shinier than usual, supposing that to be possible, thought Felicity as they twinkled back at her in the light of her roving torch.

Upstairs, I've never been upstairs, thought Felicity, at least not on one of my secret visits.

At the foot of the stairs, Felicity hesitated. They rose, steep and narrow : no angles, no turns. Even allowing for her stiff joints and slow movements, if Lily should stir from her bed, Felicity could be caught.

But it was not just that practical consideration which had prevented Felicity from venturing upstairs in the past. There was something more, an unease difficult to define. Perhaps, she told herself, it is only the feeling that while I know that the downstairs is empty, I do know that someone else is upstairs – even if asleep. She stared upwards. She had made up her mind not to bother with any more night adventures in the cottage after this one. It seemed a pity to lose this last opportunity to forage upstairs; not to take up the challenge.

The house was so quiet. Lily must be very soundly asleep. Even if she should waken, surely there would be preliminary little movements, shufflings, a turning-on of a light. Sufficient warning for Felicity to race down the stairs before Lily could reach her bedroom door. Even if she should hear me in sudden flight, thought Felicity, I would be out of sight by the time Lily would have reached the top of the stairs. If she is disturbed, then I could leave the back door wide and she would know that there really had been an intruder and that it had not been her imagination. That could be quite useful.

Quietly, treading on the inside edge of the steps in case they should creak, Felicity began her climb.

The bathroom – lavatory, basin and bath aglimmer in the moonlight – yielded no inspiration. It would be no good putting the plug in the bath and leaving the tap running – Lily could be awakened by the sound of the water.

The door of Lily's bedroom stood slightly ajar. Cautiously, Felicity pushed it wider and stealthily advanced a few steps into the room.

The curtains were not drawn. She could make out Lily's head on the pillow. A bottle gleamed on the bedside table – it looked very much like the brandy bottle that Felicity had taken from the cupboard for Lily that afternoon. Felicity could detect a smell of brandy on the air, overlaying the sweet sickly smell of Lily's cold cream. There was something else in addition to the immediately identifiable smells: something sour and unpleasant. Felicity crept a little closer to the bed. A smaller bottle lay on its side beside the brandy bottle, the top off, empty. Felicity's foot slid on something by the bed. She looked down. Vomit, and, where it had rolled to the carpet a fraction away from the revolting slimy mess, one solitary pill.

Involuntarily, Felicity retched with disgust and, appalled by the noise she had made, stood rooted to the floor waiting for Lily to move.

She stood, hand clapped over her mouth, for what seemed minutes, staring at Lily, dreading to see her eyes open. The tick of Lily's alarm-clock seemed very loud in the silence. There was no other sound, Felicity suddenly realised. Lily was making no sound at all. Felicity took her hand from her mouth and clutched at the front of her coat as the terrible significance of that silence, the brandy and the empty pill bottle suddenly dawned upon her.

She forced her legs to move. She edged away from the bed, placing one foot cautiously behind the other, never taking her eyes off the face that lay, a darker shadow on the pale glimmer of the pillow.

Felicity had almost reached the door, was groping with one hand behind her for its edge, when she thought that she did at last hear a sound from the bed. A snuffle, a movement. She hesitated briefly and then took a step forward. Her eye slid from Lily's face to see if the limbs under the bedclothes had moved. Something did seem to move down there, down at Lily's feet. There was a shadow, darker than the pools of shade on the far side of the bed where Lily's body obscured the light from the moon. Felicity swayed. The shape seemed to waver, elongate, rise.

Her legs seemed to bear Felicity of their own volition down the stairs, through the kitchen and out of the back door. She found herself standing on the step almost before she was aware of the urgent need to get away.

She banged the door shut behind her and scrabbled feverishly in her pockets for the key. It seemed important that she should lock the door behind her swiftly, imprisoning whatever it was that she believed she had seen on Lily's bed. Even as, sobbing in relief, she found the key and thrust it home in the lock, the thought overwhelmed Felicity that that dark thing, curled there on the bed, would not be contained by doors, locked or unlocked.

As she fled, plimsolls slapping with urgent rhythm across Lily's lawn and down the long brick path of Westwood's garden, she sent each gasping exhalation on its way with an explosive 'No'.

Like a wild parody of a small child playing at trains, Felicity sped on her way unaware of the sounds formed by lips and tongue. All she could hear was the pounding of her heart, filling her ears with its surge and deafening her to the tiny rustles and crepitations that stirred on every side as small creatures of the night took flight and scurried from the alarm of her noisy passage.

She had to pause for a moment before climbing up to the laundry window. A stitch gripped her side, she knew that it had clutched her at the far end of the tennis court but it was only now, almost safely home, that she dared acknowledge it. When she did eventually get herself up and through the window, she almost lost her footing on the other side. The threatened fall steadied her, brought reality into some sort of focus. She blundered through the line of damp clothes; not troubling to escape their cold touch, almost welcoming it on her hot face.

She remembered to return the key of the cottage to the board. Someone might have need of that very soon now. She had switched on her torch to locate the board and by its light saw that Puss-puss, disturbed, had come to investigate.

Felicity crouched to pick him up. He would be warm comfort when she reached her bed. She stretched out a hand. Puss-puss spat. A growl bubbled up in the cat's throat and he sprang up and sideways out of her grasp. He leapt across the room and Felicity could hear the thud of the kitchen door as he raced from her, thrusting the door wide with the impact of his rush.

Not wanting to go into the kitchen for fear of seeing again that wild glare in Puss-puss's eyes, Felicity gulped the cold water she badly needed from one of the taps over the laundry sinks. The water tasted brackish, as though it had lain too long in old, furred pipes. But it steadied her. She threw water from her cupped hands over her face. She had made such a lot of careless noise: Puss-puss had been startled. That was all. She let the cold water run over her wrists. The pain of the stitch in her side had eased, her breathing was almost normal. She concentrated fiercely on these measurable things.

Quietly Felicity mounted the stairs and marvelled that she could not even remember descending those others such a short while ago. Perhaps she really had flown. She had heard that people who fell into water could sometimes find themselves swimming although they had never learned to do so.

She got her coat off, her fingers shaking and trembling as she undid the buttons. She threw the coat on the end of her bed. The knots in the laces of her plimsolls defeated her; she levered them off, still tied, pressing her heels against the leg of her bed and glad of the solidity of the contact.

She dragged the bedclothes over her and regretted the way in which she had flung the bedding down such a short time ago, the sheets were chill and comfortless. She clicked the light off and the room was horribly dark. If she turned the light on again she would be forced to see the china cottage in too much clarity.

She slipped out of bed and flung the curtains wide, the big brass rings rattling on the old-fashioned pole.

At first the cold light seemed a comfort until she began to wonder if the pillows on her bed glimmered as had Lily's and if her own face would look as alien in light that was neither of the day nor electric.

Perhaps Lily had not been quite dead. But how could Felicity tell anyone to fetch help, how explain her being in the cottage? She bit the back of her hand. Don't think about it. Don't think about it. She had another pain now, a dragging heavy ache in her tummy. She doubled up her knees to ease it. Please, God, I didn't mean . . . I only wanted her to move to somewhere else . . . it was only a sort of game . . . pleeeese. 'Four angels round my bed,' Felicity gabbled into her pillow. 'Four angels round my bed' . . . I can't remember what comes next! Anyway, she told herself, there really isn't anyone listening, you know you don't believe there actually is. She pressed her knees tighter to her body as another cramp seized her tummy. She screwed her eyes tight shut, trying to squeeze out the visual memory of what had lain at Lily's feet. It couldn't really have been Jackie. If she concentrated hard enough she could turn it into something ordinary and possible – a sprawl of knitting perhaps, a discarded cardigan.

The cramp in her tummy eased. Cautiously, Felicity straightened her legs. The bottom of the bed still felt a little warm – so much had happened in such a short time. She sat up a little to pull the coverlet higher. And then she saw it, at the end of the bed. A congealing of shadow, a darkness curled.

Samuel heard the screaming in the corridor. For one dreadful moment, not fully awake, he thought time had slipped and Edwina ran once more through the house tearing the silence asunder. Then he heard Edith's voice and Edward's and the screaming resolved itself into the voice of Felicity.

The nightmares of childhood! Samuel turned on his side, settled his chin deeper in the pillow. Let Edward and Edith cope with it. He'd had more than his fair share of alarums in the night.

17

The big black hired car carrying the last of the few mourners back to the station glided ponderously down the drive. Edith watched it out of sight and allowed the expression, which she hoped had conveyed both dignity and a sense of occasion, to fade from her face. She had bowed as the car had drawn away from the front of Westwood; nothing excessive, just a controlled movement of the head. Anything in the nature of a wave would have seemed inappropriate.

It had really all gone off very well. But Edith was relieved that it was over and reluctant to go back into the house.

Samuel had insisted on taking charge of all the arrangements. It had been his suggestion that the handful of mourners should return to Westwood for refreshments. His manner had been impeccable, gracious and only slightly authoritarian as befitted a gentleman attending to the last rites for the relict of a family retainer. Lily's mourners had been suitably impressed. That bony, gaunt woman, thought Edith, had looked appropriate at a funeral, there had been a suggestion of the knacker's yard about her. What had been her name? Milly, that was it. 'Mil and Lil they called us – back in the good old ATS days!' That was how she had introduced herself to Edith, a mournful look in her eye and a large port in her hand. But when Milly had thanked Samuel for 'sending Lil off so lovely', Samuel's reply had not been couched in the happiest of terms – 'It was my pleasure, dear lady, my pleasure.'

Samuel had looked very handsome in his old black Vicuna – a trifle warm for the season, perhaps, but it had given him a distinctly patrician air.

Edith, her face upturned to the gentle sun, wandered a little distance from the front door. If they came looking for her then she did not want to be too quickly found.

The cousins, Ellie and Glad from Scunthorpe, had looked just like a brace of plump partridges! It had been just like Lily, they had said, to do everything in such an ordered way, even to leaving letters to all concerned. There had been the forethought, too, that had gone into the note pinned to the front door – 'Milkman, please ring the police', it had said. There had been a letter for Edith herself. It had told her what a comfort Felicity had been to Lily in the last months of her life. Well, there was no doubt that Lily had had few friends. Miss Sinclair had attended the funeral, of course, in a black straw which had seen better days. Edward had run her home earlier: she had become restless, worrying about the shop – Saturday, as she had pointed out, being one of her busiest days.

Mrs Watson had been extraordinarily co-operative, insisting on turning up to help; a little disappointed, perhaps, that the attendance had been so small. But she had behaved very nicely, relieving people of their coats at the door, handing round sandwiches and cake with an almost deferential air. She had even worn a white apron, the cut of which, Edith reflected, had been a little too institutional – more the sort of thing one would associate with an attendant in a lunatic asylum. Still, she had tried to do her best, and that was the main thing.

Edith flicked her handkerchief (which was quite dry, but anything else would have been hypocritical) over the garden seat before sitting down. She kicked off her shoes: the grass was not very damp. She closed her eyes and practised the relaxation drill she had heard on Woman's Hour, letting her face fall slack in a rather alarming manner but secure in the knowledge that she could not be overlooked. The last few days had been very trying: very trying indeed.

Felicity was the real worry. One couldn't attribute everything to the shock of that damned woman's death. No.

Felicity had had that hysterical turn before anyone had known of Lily's suicide. All that screaming about something being at the bottom of her bed! Even when Edith had pointed out to Felicity that she had left her gaberdine there (and taken the opportunity of giving her a lecture on the importance of tidiness), she had taken a lot of calming down. She had insisted on remaining for what was left of the night in her parents' bed and Edward had had to sleep in Felicity's. There was something to be said, thought Edith, circling her ankles to relieve the ache in her legs, for separate beds. One should perhaps give it thought.

But, when, the following morning, Felicity had started her period, then the whole episode fell into perspective. It could be a trying time for a girl, her first period: everyone accepted that. But the fuss Felicity had made! Weeping about the blood, quite beside herself. Iron pills, that would be the thing to give her. The poor child looked so washed out.

Life was really very tiresome. No sooner had one worry disappeared, than another took its place. Just when money was no longer going to be such an agonising problem, Felicity apparently was going to start playing up! Edith heaved a sigh. A frown puckered her face, undoing all the good of the relaxation exercise, she thought crossly, frowning harder with vexation.

Edith switched her thoughts to less irritating matters. The Vicar hadn't stayed long. Well, Lily could hardly have been considered to be a devoted parishioner and, besides, there was no love lost between the Vicar and Samuel. The Vicar had not hidden his surprise, either, that Lily had not been buried alongside her husband. Some mix-up apparently, when Gudgeon had died. Samuel had taken charge then as well (he really did have a talent for funerals) and, by some oversight, only one plot had been purchased.

Well, Lily was probably better off where she was – that pink chestnut in the far corner of the churchyard was really very pretty in the spring. Poor old Gudgeon was stuck with being far too close to old Gordon Fenn's and Dora's hideous, ornate tomb for aesthetic comfort! Still, the proximity did give him the benefit of the occasional bunch of flowers. When Samuel took it into his head to honour his parents' memory from time to time, he usually put the left-over blossoms on Gudgeon's grave. Perhaps Gudgeon, being a gardener, appreciated that touch.

Oh dear, thought Edith, easing her feet back into her shoes, I am rambling on in my mind, as though they are all somehow still here, aware of what goes on. Such nonsense! But sometimes one does fear that one is stuck with them for ever.

She ambled back to the house, pausing for one last look at the tranquillity of the front garden before reluctantly going inside. She wondered, vaguely, if Puss-puss was hiding out there somewhere under the shrubs, or perhaps in the jungle of the grounds at the back of Westwood. He'd walked out of the house a few days ago and had not come back. Well, Edith could understand that. She had often felt like doing the same thing herself; but surely things would be better from now on!

The drawing-room was already back to normal – not that that was necessarily a good thing of itself. Mrs Watson had cleared everything away with great despatch.

'Wondered where you'd got to! We've been waiting for you.' Samuel was standing on the hearthrug, a large cigar in his hand. He was bursting with exuberance. Oh dear, thought Edith, he is going to be worse in triumph than in adversity, the apparently impossible having a nasty habit of becoming nothing of the kind. Edward was looking pleased with himself, but contriving to appear sheepish at the same time.

Samuel walked over to the side window and, bending down, dragged something from where it had been concealed behind the valance of the window seat. It was a tray bearing four glasses and, in an ice-bucket which Edith had not seen in use for years, a bottle of Krug.

'My surprise!'

Samuel was positively chortling as he carried the tray to the table, holding it high, the ice tinkling against the bottle. 'Well, the days of penny-pinching, holding on, are gone for good. Here we come! I'm back in the swim of things at last!' The cork sprang from the bottle with a report that was music to Samuel's ears and flew straight towards the portrait of old James Fenn. It hit that sober man fairly and squarely on his third waistcoat button.

Samuel whooped with delight, the champagne foaming over his thick hands and fizzing to the carpet.

'Never mind, old girl!' He said, seeing Edith's appalled look. 'Soon get you a new carpet!' and he rubbed his shoe over the froth of bubbles that were rapidly sinking into the pile.

'Where's Felicity, then? Fetch her, fetch her! We must all be together – all the family.'

Felicity was, in fact, already entering the room, but so subdued was her movement that it was little wonder that she had almost escaped notice.

She really does look done-in, poor child, thought Edith noticing, too, how Felicity seemed to stumble a little as she crossed the room – it was almost as though she had tripped against something. But, of course, there was nothing there at all! Edith's eyes had gone to the floor almost expecting to see something, although she was aware that there could be nothing. Poor Felicity, a touch of dizziness, obviously. I really must get her some iron pills.

Samuel was filling the glasses. He handed one to Felicity.

'Steady on, Father, she's only a child,' demurred Edward.

'Nonsense, nonsense! Won't do her any harm. The good life, Edward, the good life – you'll have to buck your ideas up!'

Samuel raised his glass and waved it expansively at the little group that stood selfconsciously by him.

'I give you . . . the Gordon-Fenns. They can't keep us down – we always get back on top in the end!'

Felicity took a tentative sip. So this, she thought as the

bubbles tickled her palate, this is champagne. She swallowed some more in the hope that it might yet fulfil her expectation.

Samuel leaned over and topped up her glass with a wide flourish that scattered drops on his gleaming shoes.

'Drink up, Felicity! Time you started to cultivate expensive tastes, my dear. You'll learn quick enough, I'll be bound!'